Missing Links and Secret Histories

Missing Links and Secret Histories:

A Selection of Wikipedia Entries
from Across the Known Multiverse

edited by

L. Timmel Duchamp

Seattle

Aqueduct Press, PO Box 95787
Seattle, WA 98145-2787
www.aqueductpress.com

ISBN: 978-1-61976-039-4
Library of Congress Control Number: 2013936863
10 9 8 7 6 5 4 3 2 1

Cover and Book Design by Kathryn Wilham
Illustration from w:Unisphere, attributed to Uri Baruchin http://
www.flickr.com/photos/uriba/21399443/. Creative Commons
Attribution 2.0 Generic license.

Printed in the USA by Thomson-Shore Inc.

Contents

Caveat Lector; or How I Ransacked Wikipedias across the Multiverse Solely to Amuse and Edify Readers

Where would we, the postmodern human world, be without Wikipedia? That august institution of the Internet may not be absolutely reliable one hundred percent of the time (as anyone honored with an entry can probably tell you), and it may not be all-inclusive, and entries may change hourly when factions are contesting ownership of an entry with flaming keystrokes, but for now, anyway, there's just nothing like it.

Like most timely ideas, Wikipedia continually spawns a host of offspring, specialized wikis designed to pool information on topics that might be only glancingly mentioned (if that) in the capital-W Wikipedia. Besides all these children of Wikipedia, though, it is time, I feel, to acknowledge the *siblings* of Wikipedia: viz., the many Wikipedias that exist across the Multiverse. *Missing Links and Secret Histories: A Selection of Wikipedia Entries from Across the Known Multiverse* collects a sampling of entries from just a handful of these sibling Wikipedias — entries I thought might shed interesting or edifying light on the familiar narratives we know (and is some cases love) in our own small corner of the Multiverse.

Just as readers are expected to approach the capital-W Wikipedia at their own risk, so they must do with the entries herein. Whether the topic is God, the apocalypse, or relations between the infamous Dr. Moreau and the notorious Colonel Kurtz, caveat lector: the entries that follow are intended for readers' amusement and edification only. I, after all, am only the channel for the entries' transmission and claim no authority for their truthfulness or accuracy in *our* universe.

—Editor L. Timmel Duchamp, Multiverse Explorer

Mystery of the Missing Mothers

Kristin King

The Mystery of the Missing Mothers

The Mystery of the Missing Mothers is an unpublished adventure novel written by <u>Nina Herzog</u> in 1937, on the eve of World War II. It featured teen sleuth Nancy going to Iraq in search of her missing mother.

CONTENTS

History

The book was written on commission for the <u>Stratemeyer Syndicate</u> but was later rejected, and all copies were ordered destroyed. However, one copy was accidentally left in the Riverside library, only to be damaged by alluvial mud.

Plot Summary

Nancy receives a mysterious letter from her grandmother Ninhursag in Iraq. It has no stamp and is addressed in odd, angled handwriting. It says, "To Nancy, c/o her mother." But Nancy has been told her mother is dead. How then did the letter get to the United States? When Nancy shows it to her father, he grabs it out of her hand, tosses it into the fire, and cautions her not to get involved.

The next morning Nancy questions her housekeeper, Effie, who maintains that Nancy's mother is dead but lets it slip that many mothers have recently died or gone missing, including the mothers of Tom Swift, Harry Potter, and a whole host of fairy tale characters.

When Nancy questions Effie further, the housekeeper evades the question, looking frightened. Nancy notices a suspicious van leaving her driveway, with the name Stratemeyer Syndicate on it.

Nancy follows the van at high speed and trails the driver into a used bookstore. By the time she arrives, the driver has already purchased a book and run out the back door. However, the clerk informs Nancy that the book is titled A Clue in the Cuneiform, and it was published under the Ninhursag imprint.

Feeling that the two mysteries must be connected, Nancy flies to Iraq in search of relatives, Mesopotamian intellectual treasure, or both.

The remainder of the text is missing, except for the last page, which was found lying next to the book.

Ending

At the end of the story, the villain has been caught, and Nancy is lunching with her boyfriend Ted, wishing that the tablets hadn't been a hoax and vowing to steer well clear of archaeologists in the future.

Controversy Over the Ending

Nina Herzog later claimed that the Stratemeyer Syndicate rewrote the last page as part of a campaign to hide the true identity of Nancy's mother.[1] Herzog claimed there was an alternate ending to _The Mystery of the Missing Mothers_, but the earliest known copy was found long after the original publication [citation needed].

Stratemeyer Syndicate

The **Stratemeyer Syndicate** is a secret publishing company that engaged in illicit ghostwriting between 1899 and 1987. Its owner, Edward Stratemeyer, is thought to have fathered a number of famous children, including the Bobbsey Twins, Tom Swift, and the Dana Girls.

Controversy

There was a longstanding legal dispute between Edward Stratemeyer and Nina Herzog that spanned hundreds of years and crossed three continents. The particulars of the dispute have been suppressed, but they may have been over parentage or authorship.

Nina Herzog

Nina Herzog is the author of the Nanshe Adventure Tales, a virtually unknown detective series published under the Ninhursag Imprint in Iraq.

History

Herzog, the daughter of an archaeologist, escaped the World War I Mesopotamian Campaign and emigrated to the Americas, where she dated Edward Stratemeyer. The romance fell apart when Stratemeyer rejected a manuscript that he had commissioned for publication. After a particularly violent breakup, they engaged in longstanding legal disputes over the identity of Nanshe.

Descendants of Herzog claim she was murdered by the Stratemeyer Syndicate.

Ninhursag (Disambiguation)

Ninhursag refers to a Sumerian goddess, also known as Ninkharsag, Ninmah, Nintu, Mamma, Mami, Aruru, and Belet-Ili. It is also used to refer to:

1 Ninhursag (character) — Recurring character in the novels of Nina Herzog.

2 Ninhursag Imprint, a publishing brand of Enheduanna Books.

The Nanshe Adventure Tales

The **Nanshe Adventure Tales** by Nina Herzog (1850-1943) is a series of unpublished manuscripts detailing the adventures of teen sleuth Nanshe, an Iraqi socialist, as she helps her mother investigate tomb thefts.

Most copies were lost either in a mudslide or in World War I. The only remaining copy, A Clue in the Cuneiform, was unearthed in the year 2037.

See Also

- A Clue in the Cuneiform
- Nancy and the Time Tunnel
- The Mystery of the Missing Mothers (Alternate Ending)

Notes

1 Herzog, Unearthing My Texts, pp. 351-355.

References

- Autobiography: Herzog, Nina (1938). *Unearthing My Texts*. Iraq: Enheduanna Books.

A Clue in the Cuneiform

The novel **A Clue in the Cuneiform** was written in 1913 by <u>Nina Herzog</u>. It is the first of a series of <u>Nanshe Adventure Tales</u>.

CONTENTS
1 Plot Summary
2 Excerpt
3 Nanshe (Character)
4 Nanshe (God)
5 See Also

Plot Summary

The book tells the story of <u>Nanshe</u> and her mother trying to catch grave robbers who have been stealing valuable cuneiform tablets, in hopes that the tablets might explain the mysterious disappearance of Mesopotamian goddesses from Western mythologies.

One night, Nanshe awakens just in time to catch a gang of robbers from stealing two trunks full of tablets. She rouses the camp, and the robbers flee. Fortunately, Nanshe happens to be an accomplished Sumerian language expert, and she and her mother work together on translating them.

The first set of texts paint a rather muddled picture of the god and goddess genealogy and provide no hints as to the location of the missing goddesses.

The other set of texts is a <u>debate between Ninhursag and Enki</u>. It looks promising, but while Nanshe and her mother are away at luncheon, a British convoy van with the logo of the <u>Stratemeyer Syndicate</u> arrives and carries off both sets of tablets.

Although the tablets are lost, and with them the key to the mystery of the missing goddesses, Nanshe and her mother have made a great breakthrough in identifying the grave robbers. They notify the authorities, who promise to stop all British convoy vans in the future.

Leaving the mystery behind, Nanshe and her mother emigrate to the United States.

Excerpt

Over a delicious luncheon of catfish, Nanshe vented her frustration. "There are so many goddesses and they're all missing and it's impossible to tell how they fit together!"

Her mother said wryly, "It's just primordial goddess muck, isn't it? Let's see... In the beginning there was no earth, no sky, no ocean, but only the primordial muck. Later the goddesses came to be named and to bear fruit. Ki, goddess of Earth, mated with An, god of Sky. Then nobody talked about them. Nammu, Sea, who woke up Enki. Maybe Nammu was Ninhursag, who maybe was once Ki, and maybe was later Ninmah or Nimennah."

"Exactly!" complained Nanshe. "All these old stories contradict themselves."

Nina commented, "They contradict themselves because the stories and the gods and goddesses themselves had to be perpetually recreated. Temples kept on sinking into the sand, and people had to rebuild them again and again. One good flood could wipe out a temple—a whole city."

"Good thing people were there to help rebuild," commented Nanshe.

"Until mankind itself became the flood," said Nina. "Until the cities grew so rich with grain and oil that invaders came to slaughter every last man, woman, and child; and to take the temples for their own. Until the goddesses retreated into the clay and sand."

"But!" said Nanshe excitedly. "Not just the clay and sand! They retreated into the *cuneiform tablets themselves!*"

Nina put down her spoon and thought. "Then that's where we hunt," she said.

Nanshe (Character)

Nanshe (character) refers to a character in the adventure novels of <u>Nina Herzog</u>, an amateur Iraqi archaeologist who was much inspired by the unearthing and translation of Mesopotamian cuneiform tablets.

Nanshe (God)

Nanshe refers to the daughter of the Sumerian gods Ninhursag and Enki. She was initially given dominion over the Persian Gulf and looked after fish and wildlife. Between 2144 and 2124 BCE she took on a new role and became wildly popular as the god of social justice. In that role, she looked out for "the widows and the orphans," standardized weights and measures, and ensured equitable distribution of food in her temples. After her heyday she faded into obscurity, although some claim that her memory lived on in other, later goddesses, such as Lady Justice.

The <u>Hymn to Nanshe</u> lays out her role and the day-to-day running of her temple.

Excerpts from the Hymn to Nanshe

1   "If the grain does not suffice for these rites and the vessels are empty and do not pour water, the person in charge of the regular offerings does not receive extra."

2   "For a susbu priest who serves his term administering food allotments and against whom a complaint has been lodged... further rations are denied and thereby mother Nance's ordinances will become apparent."

See Also

- Mystery of the Missing Mothers
- Nancy and the Time Tunnel

Nancy and the Time Tunnel

Nancy and the Time Tunnel by Nina Herzog (2037) is an unpublished novel that tells the story of Nancy investigating her missing mother and finding a mudslide in the Riverside library, which leads to her discovery of a time tunnel that changes Nancy's life forever.

The appendix includes an alternate ending for the novel Mystery of the Missing Mothers.

CONTENTS

Plot Summary

Nancy and her friend Tom Swift are comparing memories about their dead mothers and discover startling similarities. Hunting for some answers, Nancy goes to the Riverside Library only to find the river has flooded and alluvial mud is swamping the library. The archaeology section is blocked off, and the nearby carpet is stained rust-brown. The librarian forbids Nancy to investigate, but Nancy is intrigued. She pulls a pair of rubber rain boots out of her knitting bag and carefully steps through the oozing and squelching mud into a dark corner. She trips, falls into a wall, and knocks a brick loose, revealing a hidden passage. Excited, Nancy pries away the bricks with a chisel she brought just in case and then goes on down the tunnel using a flashlight she just happened to have.

Midway through the tunnel, Nancy hears a noise. She turns to see the librarian in hot pursuit. Nancy flees, but the librarian catches up to her and explains that she is really Nina Herzog, the author, and that this tunnel will take them to a Sumerian city circa 2100 B.C.E.

When they step out, Nancy is thunderstruck by the size of the city and also quite shocked at the dark complexions of the people around her. Nina takes Nancy to a performance of Sumerian debate poetry, a <u>debate between Ninhursag and Enki</u>.

After the performance, Nancy sees <u>Edward Stratemeyer</u> fleeing the scene with cuneiform tablets in his hands. She alerts the temple guards, who capture him and return the tablets to their rightful owners. Unfortunately, he escapes and flees to the time tunnel! Nancy and Nina pursue him, but he zooms away from the library in a <u>Stratemeyer Syndicate</u> van.

Admitting defeat—for now—Nina takes Nancy out to luncheon, where Nina explains a few plot points and sheds some light on Nancy's parentage. Nancy decides to put the information to good use as a detective. She bids farewell to Nina, promising to visit often.

Debate Between Ninhursag and Enki

The "debate poem" or "contest poem" is a form of Sumerian literature in which, two rivals argue about which is the best, each bragging and each insulting the other. The god Enlil decides the "winner" and then reconciles the rivals. The most famous is the <u>debate between Hoe and Plough</u>.

In the **debate between Ninhursag and Enki**, the two gods argue to determine which character is better and more deserving of passing on into the future: Nanshe or Nancy. Unfortunately, the part of the tablets that declare the winner was driven over by a van and utterly destroyed.

Ninhursag: "Your Nancy is only a cardboard cutout of a person. She has no self-doubt, fears, or social blunders."

Enki: "Who cares about that, when she has such a fast car! My Nancy can fly through the lands and none can catch her. She can squirm out of any tight place. Truly Nisaba watches over her.

Meanwhile your goddess has to go around on her own two feet, slow and plodding like a mule."

Ninhursag: "Your detective doesn't do anything important, she's good for nothing, all she does is save jewels for rich people, and she doesn't praise the goddesses, and she even insults the black-headed people. My god looks out for widows and orphans and beggars, and if rich people try to take the temple offerings meant to be shared, she boots them right out. If she walks on two feet it is because she is truly with the people and does not scorn them or attempt to speed past them in a smelly old chariot."

Enki: "No, your goddess wasn't worth anything even in her times of glory, she was just a minor deity in one little temple, and if it weren't for those buried tablets, nobody would remember her at all. My Nancy is a folk hero whose name will live on so long as there are criminals to catch."

Ninhursag: "My goddess was praised far and wide, and if it weren't for her watching over the Gulf, nobody would have had anything to eat, and the entire Sumerian civilization would have died out, and that means there wouldn't have been any writing and Western civilization would consist entirely of barbarians."

Enki: "You're exaggerating."

Excerpt

The following **excerpt** appeared in Nancy and the Time Tunnel, an unpublished novel written in 2037 by Nina Herzog.

"Well, who is this Nanshe character who appears in A Clue in the Cuneiform?" Nancy asked.

"Okay, so here's one version of the story," said Nina. "I birthed her, because I wrote about her, and she is an *earlier* version of you. I picked up a piece of cuneiform, and there was just a little piece of goddess attached, so I wrote her into an adventure. And then the war started, and I fled to the U.S., and then Edward Stratemeyer got hold of my manuscript and used it as a basis for his mystery novels, which is something we've been fighting about ever since."

"Slow down," said Nancy. "If you birthed her, did you birth me? Are you my mother?"

"Okay," said Nina. "I wrote some stories about Nanshe, and then Edward thought he could sell them for fifty cents a book, so he made you up, but when I tried to write a book about you, he set the Syndicate on me."

"He's my father?" asked Nancy.

"Well, hang on. There's another version of the story, and for that you have to go on back to my parents, Ninhursag and Enki. They were gods, and they birthed the human race so we could build their canals and temples and tell their stories. They made me, you, and Edward Stratemeyer."

"Are you my sister?" asked Nancy.

"Exactly!"

"And also—my mother?"

"Just so, Nancy. I'm the mother of all the motherless adventure heroes. I watch over all of them, but not *too* closely. I let them get into danger, and then I haul them out as needed. And I'd actually be in the stories—theirs and yours too—if it weren't for the Stratemeyer Syndicate perpetually editing me out."

"Well, Mom, I'm delighted to meet you!"

Nancy and her mother spent the afternoon catching up, and then Nancy caught the first plane to Iraq. The two of them were fated to meet again soon, in the exciting sequel Search for Stratemeyer. But that is a story for another day.

The Mystery of the Missing Mothers
(Alternate Ending)

Author Nina Herzog claimed that the following **alternate ending** belonged to her unpublished novel, The Mystery of the Missing

<u>Mothers</u>. However, the earliest known copy was found a hundred years later, in the appendix to <u>Nancy and the Time Tunnel.</u> [citation needed]

"Nancy will never in a million years believe that she is really the granddaughter of a Sumerian goddess," complained George, sipping an after-dinner drink at the Riverside hotel.

"I know," said Ninhursag, leaning back and puffing on a pipe. "That's hard for a two-dimensional cardboard cutout to take in. Still, if even one copy of this manuscript survives, we will have done our job."

"How can you say that?" Bess asked in despair. "Everything is lost. All the goddesses, all the mothers, everything."

"Not really," said Ninhursag. "Everything changes, dies, transforms, and lives in some other way. If this is all we can get, so be it. The original Nancy will form the basis of a century of girls growing up to think that women can be powerful."

"We already know that," said Bess.

"True," said Ninhursag. "But you will forget it. War is coming, a world war, and everything you know will be drowned in a flood of soldiers. Take my advice and hang tight in a book for a while. As for me, I'm heading off to the primordial muck for a century-long nap."

See Also

- The Mystery of the Missing Mothers
- A Clue in the Cuneiform
- Edward Stratemeyer <http://en.wikipedia.org/wiki/Edward_Stratemeyer>
- Enki <http://en.wikipedia.org/wiki/Enki>
- Nanshe <http://en.wikipedia.org/wiki/Nanshe>
- Ninhursag <http://en.wikipedia.org/wiki/Ninhursag>
- Stratemeyer Syndicate <http://en.wikipedia.org/wiki/Stratemeyer_Syndicate>

Additional Resources

- The Debate Between Hoe and Plough <http://etcsl.orinst.ox.ac.uk/cgi-bin/etcsl.cgi?text=t.5.3.1&charenc=j#>
- Enheduanna: The First Known Author <http://www.atanet.org/publications/beacons_10_pages/page_15.pdf >
- The Electronic Text Corpus of Sumerian Literature < http://etcsl.orinst.ox.ac.uk/ >
- A Hymn to Nance <http://etcsl.orinst.ox.ac.uk/cgi-bin/etcsl.cgi?text=t.4.14.1&charenc=j#>

The Five Petals of Thought

Nisi Shawl

The Five Petals of Thought

The Five Petals of Thought, aka **the New Bedford Rose**, refers to a philosophical system dating back to the late-eighteenth and early-nineteenth centuries, which was widely adopted by activists in Anglophone countries, primarily the US and, to some extent, Great Britain.[1]

Within this article "the Five Petals" and "the Rose" are sometimes used as shortened versions of the system's full name.

CONTENTS

Introduction

Elements and Structures

The Five Petals of the New Bedford Rose represent Thought, Action (also called "pre-action" and "pro-action"), Observation, Integration, and New Action (also called "re-action"). Thought is the first step in any course. The first petal is thus associated with visualizations, dreams, and all other methods of forming concepts. Action is next; its alternative names of pre-action and pro-action refer to the idea that any action taken will serve as a prequel or prologue to another action. Observation occurs both during and after Action, and provides material for Integration into the original concept. Integration then leads to New Action.[2]

Many followers of the New Bedford Rose stipulate its application as cyclical in nature, saying that New Action should be followed again by Observation, Integration, and further New Action.[citation needed]

African Influences

Descendants of formerly enslaved Africans are among the earliest proponents of the Five Petals,[citation needed] but controversy surrounds the assertion that African-based philosophies underlie them. Skye, writing in the most popular book on the subject, *The Five Petals of Thought*, uses several Yoruba, Igbo, and other West African words and phrases. Primary sources appear to ignore them in favor of European-derived terminology. This could be attributed to cultural deracination, or it could mean that originally there was no such connection.

Asian Influences

Despite comparisons to the Five Elements philosophies of China and Japan and parallels in Hinduism and related East Indian religions, no direct path can be traced between these traditions and the Five Petals.

American Influences and Others

Strong evidence exists that members of South Carolina's Lumbee tribe participated in the founding of the Five Petals community on Harker Island.[3] However, too-great assimilation combined with the subsequent near-erasure of Lumbee cultural identity makes it impossible to assess the degree to which the philosophy borrowed from Lumbee or other indigenous traditions.

Due to the undeniable presence of formerly-indentured Irish and English and other immigrants[citation needed] in the Harker Island, North Carolina community and throughout the history of the Five Petals, European influence on the philosophy's systematization is safe to assume, though controversial in its extent.

History

Harker Island

As recounted in Elvira Coker's 1858 memoir *The Three Rivers*, this was the site of the philosophy's first Utopian community. A large contingent from an inland village of Lumbees joined forces with manumitted black slaves and formerly-indentured whites. Coker claims the community operated according to the Five Petals system between its 1755 founding and its dissolution in 1816. Nothing in local records contradicts her assertions, and though she admits that she could have been little more than a child, and then only during the community's final years, her detailed and colorful account is all modern historians have to draw on. A sample:

Aunt Abby spoke to all of us gathered there like a Gypsy princess, gazing into the heart of the bonfire like looking in a crystal ball, telling all our futures. We [were] to fly all over the country, as [if we were] little birds or spinning seeds, or drops of water from a big wave, or sparks from that selfsame fire. Oh, it was poetry! Her black hair was whipping around in the wind, and her pretty glass beads were shining and I wanted to be her.

Responding apparently to threats of violence by those surrounding them, the community split up, with "Aunt Abby" (Abigail Day), her brother Pursell, and a few others traveling to New Bedford's manufactories.

Ramblin School

The 1833 lease for the grounds and buildings originally housing the Ramblin School is the earliest historical record of the existence of the Five Petals of Thought. Louanne Gonder, with the financial backing of her sister "Bee" (Carlotta Beatrice Day), founded the school. A prospectus from its early years promises "training in the principles of the New Bedford Rose for young girls about to enter employment or marriage."

The school continued operation until its closure during the second wave of the influenza epidemic of 1918. Though in August of that year staff appeared unaffected by the disease, administrators deemed it prudent not to open and risk exposure and possible infection.[4]

Civil War and Reconstruction

It was during the US Civil War that Ramblin School and the Rose as a whole first became closely identified with medicine and nursing.[citation needed] Resistance to white supremacist backlash during Reconstruction helped spread and popularize its teachings.[1] Five Petals teachings are credited with preventing the destruction of Wilmington, North Carolina's black majority.[3]

The Great War

Unwilling to fight as soldiers, followers of the Five Petals found themselves forced to ally with religious Conscientious Objectors, usually Quakers and Christadelphians.[1] Mass sentiment turned against them as pacifism became equated in the public's mind with cowardice, and the dissolution of Ramblin School during this period seemed to confirm the movement's death.

Depression-Era Efforts

Despite the economic downturn most of the US experienced in the 1930s, or perhaps because of it, the Five Petals flourished.[2] Establishing farms and cottage industries that dealt in trade items reminiscent of those produced long ago on Harker Island, Five Petals communities sprang up throughout New England and the Great Lakes Region. Brooms, crockery, blankets, and similarly simple household goods supplemented farm produce offered to individuals and institutions at prices they evidently found affordable.[5]

Somewhat sparser but still noteworthy Rose distribution could be found in the Northwest, with one community (Black Diamond) forming in Idaho.[6]

The success of these business efforts was attributed by adherents to the correctness of the Five Petals philosophy; their enthusiasm and the system's rising popularity averted the collapse that had once seemed inevitable.[2]

Pacifism and "Women's work"

Participation in the "just" war against Nazism proved even more difficult to resist than in previous conflagrations.

Drawing on farming, crafting, medical, and educational expertise, and putting to use their well-honed skills in social organizing, those who practiced the Five Petals made themselves indispensable to the military in a variety of noncombat roles.[1] Some of these practitioners were women, and the rest were men unafraid of so-called women's work, which reinforced in the men charged with recruiting soldiers the idea of their unfitness for service, at least at first. Avowed and ascribed sexual proclivities also tended to exempt Five Petals adherents from military duty.[2] In many cases earlier ties to pacifistic religions were reaffirmed; through various strategies all WWII's 640,000-plus active followers of the New Bedford Rose in the US, Canada, Great Britain, Australia, and New Zealand managed to escape combat.[1]

On the "Home Front," Five Petals organizers launched study groups and established cooperative nurseries, causing former homemakers to seriously consider the movement's philosophy. Often this consideration ended in their becoming new members.[2]

In contrast to the deleterious effects of WWI, adherent numbers rose slightly during this period, and outsider opinion of the Five Petals significantly improved.[1]

Red and Pink

After WWII, with very few exceptions, the influence of the Five Petals of Thought shrank. Certain labor unions remained true to their roots, but many more capitulated to increasingly entrenched corporate interests; anti-communist sentiments and cries of "Pinko!" eradicated the most recent gains in popularity.[1] Exceptions to the general disaffection included the East Village community, insulated perhaps by its sophisticated urban surroundings[2] and, conversely, the farm on Whalen Island in Oregon's Sandlake Estuary.[citation needed]

It is during this period, due most likely to the influence of the Beats or Beatniks, that the Five Petals became associated with Asian philosophy.[2]

Despite the above exceptions, the Rose was again quiescent for some time.

Black Power and Blacklight

The Civil Rights Movement provided followers of the Five Petals philosophy with a natural field of exercise. The Reverend Dr. King's covert espousal of their methods is now well known; after his death in 1970, and in concert with protestors' radicalization, acceptance grew wider and wider. Student opposition to the Vietnam War fed off this pool of activism and fed into it. Countercultural acceptance of the Five Petals of Thought blossomed, so to speak. [1] Much of the philosophy's current preservation is owing to its expansion during that time. This, in turn, has helped its current resurgence.

Adherents

Early Practitioners

Though its origins were highly localized, the Five Petals quickly spread to become a global phenomenon. Early followers include Dorothy Gale, initially a Kansan but eventually a Queen of Oz.[citation needed] Two others from roughly the same period were British citizens: Wendy Darling and Jean Muir (Lady Coventry). Darling learned the principles of the New Bedford Rose some time after the girlhood Barrie chronicled,[citation needed] but Muir stated emphatically that she owed the crowning success of her acting career, the performance that won her Sir John's marriage proposal, solely to her application of the Five Petals of Thought.[7]

Unacknowledged Adherents

In times of the movement's retreating influence few admitted to studying the Five Petals, much less espousing them.[1] Still, skilled detective work reveals that among those who must have owed much to the Five Petals philosophy was Mardou Fox. Her carefully cryptic diary reflects the period's lack of openness, yet tells more of her internal states than Beat author Jack Kerouac manages to convey in his booklength account of their love affair. Repeated appointments with "Missy C." and "Doctor Dee" indicate that she met with code-named activist organizers now understood to have been deeply involved in the Rose's recruitment efforts.[8]

Other possible secret adherents under investigation include Claudine Willy and Emma Peel.[citation needed]

Current Celebrity Practitioners

Today's accepting atmosphere means that open avowals of support for the Five Petals of Thought are common. Geneticist Shori Ina, "retired" rock star Hollis Henry, high-powered LA agent Angela Toussaint, and hacker Marcus Yallow, to name just a few, are all Five Petals proponents. A longer list is available on the movement's website.

Rediscovery

The immensely successful popular psychology book *The Five Petals of Thought* by Melissa Skye is undoubtedly responsible for the resurgence of the activist philosophy for which it was named. Though it wasn't published till 2005, Skye has stated in an online interview that she'd worked on the book's manuscript for over a decade (eleven years) and that her interest in the topic started developing even earlier. This was in part due to her descent from several of the philosophy's founders.

Translated into twenty languages and also offered in multiple audiobook formats *The Five Petals of Thought* mainly focuses on personal applications of the philosophy. A brief history section relies heavily on quotations from the works of Coker, "Dee," and other firsthand participants, and a short chapter speculates on things impossible to determine, such as the philosophy's ontological roots in the remnants of its first proponents' African belief systems.[9]

To date more than 100 million copies of *The Five Petals of Thought* have sold worldwide.[10]

Related Movements

Feminism

The fight for women's suffrage in the US and other Anglophone countries may have begun independently of any influence of the Five Petals, but this seems unlikely, given the Rose's long association with egalitarianism and its tradition of overwhelmingly feminine leadership. Certainly the suffrage movement's relatively easy victories in countries where the Five Petals were well established leads one to conclude that the struggle might have been longer and more bitter without their help.[11]

Conversely, feminism has obviously offered Observations to be Integrated by the Rose's practitioners.[citation needed]

Socialism

The many sorts of socialism embraced by followers of the Five Petals both proves the connection between the two movements and highlights how one didn't necessarily lead to the other. Predating the First International by decades,[1] the Harker Island settlement may be viewed as a sort of proto-Socialist experiment. But as a philosophy and methodology for creating change rather than a fixed method of redistributing economic benefits, the New Bedford Rose differs from all forms of socialism on a very basic level. It could be said that the Five Petals are a way of _using_ socialism.

Notes/References

1   Poundstone, Meaghan (June 16, 2011). "A Brief Online History of Activism," www.misible.com.

2   Vandeleur, Nora (ed.) (1976). _The Front Inside: Missives from "Missy C.,"_ Beherenow Books.

3   Gowen, Samuel and Gunther Wilkins (1982). _The Only Land We Know,_ Arborea Press.

4 Scanned and digitized files of the <u>New Bedford Historical Society</u>.

5 Traynor, Blake and August Sillough (2002). <u>"Transcontinental Institutional Purchasing Patterns in Response to Depression-Era Economic Considerations: Necessity vs. Convention"</u> in _Explorations in Economic History_, v 11, #3, September.

6 Calloway, Ruby (1951). _Kootenai, My Kootenai_, Kootenai Historical Library.

7 Barnard, A.M. (ed.) (1909). <u>_Letters and Other Indiscretions_</u>, Concord House.

8 Fox, Mardou (1960). _My Blues Ain't Like Yours_, Grove Press.

9 <u>"Ain't I a Woman?"</u> (May 2007). Interview with Melissa Skye at <u>Wordforth</u>.

10 Bowker "PubEasy" statistics for March 2013, www.bowker.com.

11 Boston Women's Educational Collective (1990). _Messy Edges: Overlapping Influences in Feminism_, BWEC.

Other Resources

- _The Three Rivers_ by Elvira Coker, 1858, Tannin and Sweete.
- _The Five Petals of Thought_ by Melissa Skye, 2005, Indigo Books.
- <u>"Excerpts from the Diaries of 'Doctor Dee'"</u> www.digitidiaries.edu.

Thaddeus P. Reeder

Jeremy Sim

[Redirected from Dear Reader]

(!) This article has multiple issues. Please help improve it or discuss these issues on the talk page.

> * It needs additional citations for verification. Tagged since November 2011.

> * It may contain original research. Tagged since November 2011.

Thaddeus Plimpwharton Reeder (1815-1881)[1] was an English governor and philanthropist, best known for being the original "Dear Reader" addressed in the texts of various Victorian-era novels. [2] His influence is best seen in the works of novelists Charlotte Brontë and Victor Hugo, though recent academic speculation has traced his impact to include modern literature as well.[1]

CONTENTS

Early Life

Thaddeus Reeder was born in <u>Bradford, Yorkshire</u> in 1815 to wealthy parents Peter and Ellen Reeder. As a child, he was described as "a blessedly slow learner" by his teacher Anne Wellington, who reportedly struggled to teach him even the most rudimentary facts of history.[2] At the age of 9, Thaddeus became acquainted with the Brontë sisters and quickly formed a friendship with <u>Charlotte</u>, <u>Emily</u>, <u>Anne</u> and their two elder sisters Maria and Elizabeth. Thaddeus was reportedly unable to distinguish between the five Brontë sisters,[3] calling them by their names interchangeably until Maria and Elizabeth died of tubercolosis in 1825, simplifying matters.

As a teenager, Thaddeus reportedly enjoyed simple joys like singing and dancing. According to his mother, he was a "kindhearted, clumsy boy" with "not a prickle to him."[3] His parents kept him out of school, concerned for their son's ability to keep up with the other students. He was known to spend hours perusing picture books in his father's library, struggling with the longer passages, and several written accounts detail the attempts of Thaddeus's friends and family to explain simple concepts and situations to him. "The boy is denser than a stone," wrote Peter Reeder in 1826.[4]

By all accounts, Thaddeus was not troubled by his personal handicaps, and lived a happy, fulfilling childhood. It was during this time that the first records appear of Thaddeus acquiring the nickname "Reeder."[5]

Dear Reader

A long-argued point of contention among scholars was put to rest when an early manuscript of the novel <u>Jane Eyre</u> was found in 2009,[1,3] bearing a preface that reads:

> To my dear friend Reeder: I dedicate this private book to you, a narrative in which the protagonist, Jane, endures many trials. I hope you enjoy it.

Reeder is addressed many times throughout the incomplete Reeder manuscript, ostensibly by the character Jane Eyre herself, explaining various plot points and background details:

> In those days, Reeder, this now narrow catalogue of accomplishments, would have been held tolerably comprehensive.

> While he is so occupied, I will tell you, Reeder, what they are.

> This is a gentle delineation, is it not, Reeder?

And arguably the most famous line in the novel:

> Reeder, I married him.[5]

Reeder/Reader Controversy

Besides the earliest manuscripts, however, all known copies of Jane Eyre address the "reader" rather than Reeder himself. Several theories have been put forth to explain the change. These include:

- Manuscript copying error.

- A falling-out between Charlotte and Reeder, perhaps precipitated by Charlotte's budding romance with her future husband Arthur Bell Nicholls.

- An authorial decision by Charlotte to avoid confusion with Jane's adoptive family in the novel, who bear the surname Reed.[6]

- Publisher pressure.[6]

Some theories hold that Charlotte was persuaded by an adult Reeder to make the changes, to avoid public embarrassment. According to these theories she did so angrily, changing the fictional Reed family into a family of unpleasant villains in reprisal.[6]

Influence on *The Hunchback of Notre Dame* and Others

The enormous success of <u>Jane Eyre</u> attracted the attention of contemporary writers such as <u>Stendhal</u>[7] and the French poet and novelist <u>Victor Hugo</u>.[8] It is reported that Hugo spent weeks poring over the manuscript, trying to ascertain the Englishwoman's secret to success. It is speculated that Hugo chose to appropriate some of Brontë's techniques for his upcoming novel *Notre-Dame de Paris*, known in English as <u>*The Hunchback of Notre-Dame*</u>.[3]

Hugo, however, was not accustomed to the Reeder technique, which involved the insertion of numerous mundane facts and explanations throughout the novel. Literary analysts have pointed to Hugo's unfamiliar use of the Reeder technique to explain a slight but perceptible rise in the abrasiveness of Hugo's narrator throughout *The Hunchback of Notre-Dame*.[8] Hugo's impatience with the ponderousness of the technique is evident from the very beginning of the novel, where he repeatedly reminds the reader of established plot details:

> The reader has, perhaps, not forgotten the impudent beggar, who at the commencement of the prologue perched himself beneath the fringe of the Cardinal's gallery.
>
> [...]
>
> The reader has not perhaps forgotten that part of the Cour des Miracles was enclosed by the ancient wall surrounding the Ville.
>
> [...]
>
> The reader has, perhaps, not forgotten that Quasimodo, the moment before he perceived the nocturnal band of the Vagabonds, while surveying Paris from the top of his tower, had discovered but a single light, which illumined a window in the uppermost floor of a lofty and gloomy building by the gate of St. Antoine.

Hugo continues in this way until the latter half of the book, where his frustration becomes more evident:

The reader already knows that this is the tower which commands a view of the Hôtel-de-Ville.

[...]

The reader probably recollects the critical situation in which we left Quasimodo.

[...]

Now, let such of our readers as are capable of generalising an image and an idea, to adopt the phraseology of the present day, permit us to ask if they have formed a clear conception of the spectacle presented, at the moment to which we are calling their attention, by the vast parallelogram of the great hall of Paris.[9]

The Reeder technique and its variants have since been used to varying degrees of success by authors like <u>Laurence Sterne</u>, <u>Adam Bede</u> and <u>Charles Dickens</u>.[7]

The Reeder Technique

The term "Reeder technique" was first used in 2011 to describe a type of literary narrator who intrudes upon the narrative to explain various terms and background details pertaining to the story. The use of the term is still the subject of much debate.

Death and Legacy

Reeder died in London in 1881, at the age of 66, leaving behind two sons and a daughter. In modern times, the concept of a "dear reader" or "gentle reader" has become emblematic of Victorian literature and is commonly used to elicit the associated hallmarks of that age. The Reeder technique is still used by writers of all types, notable in modern-day works such as <u>Italo Calvino's</u> *<u>If On a Winter's Night a Traveler</u>* and <u>Lemony Snicket's</u> *<u>A Series of Unfortunate Events</u>*.

A <u>Dear Reader letter</u> is a type of letter in which the writer introduces himself or herself as if addressing an unacquainted stranger.

Notes/References

1 Himmsler, M., *Great Techniques of Victorian Literature*, Medallion, 2010. ISBN 0974655910.

2 *The Times* 2 August 1923.

3 Pennyworth Kent G., "The Reeder Legacy," *Specula*, 47 (2009): 289-95.

4 Brontë, Charlotte, "A Story of a Girl Named Jane Eyre." Manuscript.From Library of Congress, *The Brontë Papers*, 501-1059.

5 Reeder, Peter, "Personal Notes." Diary. From Library of Congress, *The Brontë Papers*, 2354-97.

6 Guzman, J., "Reeder: Fact or Fiction?" *Specula*, <u>49 (2010): 101-23.</u>

7 <u>Pennyworth, Kent G., *Advances in Literature of the 16th Century*, Lyons, 2009. ISBN 9780974655963.</u>

8 Pennyworth Kent G., "The Reeder Effect in *Notre-Dame de Paris*," *Specula*, 50 (2010): 26-49.

9 Hugo, Victor, *The Hunchback of Notre-Dame*, 1831.

See Also

- Second-person narrative
- Unreliable narrator
- Victorian literature

The Gimmerton Theory

Nick Tramdack

Gimmerton Theory

The Gimmerton Theory is a controversial attempt to account for the whereabouts of Heathcliff during his absence from Wuthering Heights between 1780 and 1783. Its most notable claim is that Heathcliff worked as a spy for the French Government under the alias of "Gimmerton." Until 2012, mainstream scholars almost universally dismissed the Gimmerton Theory as a fabrication. However, the recent rediscovery of the Marquis de Sade's so-called V Manuscript has spurred a critical reevaluation not only of Heathcliff's history, but of Sade's most famous biographical subjects, Justine and Juliette de Lorsagne, as well.

CONTENTS
1 Background
2 W. B. Yeats and the Gimmerton Theory
3 The Order of the Golden Dawn
4 The V Manuscript
5 Excerpt
6 Conclusion
7 Notes/References
8 See Also

Background

Upon noted antiquarian Sir John Lockwood's death from gout in 1847, his personal papers were acquired and published by Emily Brontë. Though initial readers considered Wuthering Heights to be a work of fiction, multiple reported sightings of Heathcliff and Catherine Earnshaw wandering the Yorkshire moors in 1886 and 1889 sparked a public sensation and renewed interest in WH.

It was only in 1926 that Bloomsbury Group member C.P. Sanger established a reliable timeline[1] for the events of WH based on the holidays and moon phases mentioned in the text. However, Sanger's ground-breaking study provided no clues to the whereabouts of Heathcliff after his flight from the Heights in 1780, or the means by which the once-penniless youngster returned to Wuthering Heights "in dress and manners a gentleman"[2] in September 1783.

W. B. Yeats and the Gimmerton Theory

The case of Heathcliff's missing three years is reported to have fascinated Irish poet, playwright, and mystic W. B. Yeats. His 1927 article "The Fortunes of Heathcliff in France"[3] expanded on Sanger's chronology. In it, Yeats claimed that upon fleeing the Heights in 1780, Heathcliff traveled to London, where he assumed the alias of Gimmerton—the town nearest to the Heights—and worked as a messenger and lookout for French spy François Henri de la Motte.

In January 1781, de la Motte was arrested and charged with reporting British fleet movements to France. Along with "Gimmerton," who was suspected of being his accomplice, he was held in the Tower of London until July, when he was convicted of treason and hanged.[4] But Gimmerton—defended *pro bono* by C.J. Stryver and Sydney Carton—was cleared of all charges and freed.

Afterwards, Yeats claimed, Heathcliff made his way to the Netherlands and then to France, where on the strength of his association with de la Motte he was welcomed as a guest into the house of Jean-Baptiste Dorval, a noted libertine and thief of the *Ancien Régime*. Dorval soon took a shine to the fierce Englishman, and it was as this man's guest that Heathcliff became experienced in polite conversation, sexual pleasures, and ultimately, robberies of mail coaches, casinos, and private estates.

Working under Dorval, Heathcliff was able to amass, by early 1783, a personal fortune amounting to nearly two hundred thousand *livres*. This money, Yeats claimed, allowed Heathcliff to live in style and adopt the title "de Hurlevent"—but he was unable to suppress his passion for Catherine and finally returned to England with the intention of winning her back.

As evidence, Yeats cited contemporary accounts of the de la Motte trial, reproducing reports of Gimmerton's physical appearance— "a brooding creature, whose fearsome aspect recalls the thieving Gypsy no less than the mongrel Lascar, and at whose sight any true-blooded Englishman cannot help but shudder"[5]—which convincingly matched physical descriptions of Heathcliff in the WH text.

However, because Yeats' claim that Heathcliff had visited France was based only on "manuscript evidence in a private collection which I hope may as soon as possible see print." critics remained less than persuaded. To make matters worse, this manuscript evidence remained unpublished for unexplained reasons, and after Yeats' death in 1939, the once-respected Gimmerton Theory fell into increasing disfavor.

The Order of the Golden Dawn

In 2012, a library of rare books, including early seventeenth-century Kabbalistic esoterica and alchemical treatises as well as Enlightenment-period erotic writings, appeared in an English estate auction. Experts now agree that this cache of rare texts originally belonged to the Stella Matutina, the branch of the Order of the Golden Dawn to which Yeats belonged. It was probably[citation needed] Yeats' research in their secret archive that had allowed him to discover the link between Heathcliff and France—but by the time he published his article in 1927, he had already left the Stella Matutina and lost all access to the very document that could have proven his claim—the V Manuscript of the Marquis de Sade.

The V Manuscript

Written by <u>Donatien Alphonse François, *Marquis de Sade*</u> in 1783 while imprisoned in the <u>Château de Vincennes,</u> this tightly written manuscript records an interview between Sade and a gentleman named "de Hurlevent" in an adjoining chamber. At first, Sade writes, the gentleman remained taciturn, but out of boredom (or perhaps, some scholars believe, the offer of political favors)[6] de Hurlevent eventually related to the Marquis the history of his wanderings in Europe in an "adequate, though imperfect French." Scholars agree that manuscript evidence confirms that Heathcliff and Hurlevent were, in fact, the same person.

Sade writes that despite his lucrative thieving partnership with <u>Dorval,</u> "Hurlevent" remained unhappy in France. Unable to forget Catherine, whom he had last seen declaring her intention to marry <u>Edgar Linton</u>, he asked Dorval for help forming a plan of action to win her back. But the gentleman thief pleaded ignorance in matters of love. ("The good Dorval preferred to pay!" was Heathcliff's remark.) Instead, Dorval suggested that he "pay a call on a certain lady of his acquaintance, whom he declared to be perfectly acquainted with every particular of seduction and vice."

Excerpt

I presented Dorval's compliments to Madame la Comtesse and, after introducing myself, explained the situation at Wuthering Heights.

"I have only one question, sir," <u>Juliette de Lorsagne</u> began, extending her little finger while sipping her chocolate. "Has your Cathy read the letters of <u>Pamela Andrews</u>?"

I replied that a copy had been in the Lintons' library at <u>Thrushcross Grange</u>.

"If that is the case, I must inform you, my friend, that 'tis impossible she will wait for you."

"But Pamela was true to her heart," I protested. "Do I not have the right to hope, madame, for—"

"On the contrary!" Juliette interrupted. "Thanks to that wretched Jesuit, the <u>Abbé Prevost</u>, we are more than familiar with Pamela here in France—and 'tis nothing more than the story of a foolish squire who, insufficiently libertine to simply ravish the maid, was duped by the saucy jade into becoming a husband. Ah, Hurlevent, Pamela's seeming reluctance to confess to coveting <u>Squire B——</u>'s great fortune merely proves that she was too bright to commit her schemes to paper; doubtless she feared her letters would be intercepted, as indeed they were...

"But recall, my friend, how shrewdly Pamela manipulates the old sot, feeding the fires of his lust—now coy, now distant; now pert, now reserved; so that while Squire B—— believed himself to be seducing her, the one being seduced was him! Nay, sir, young Pamela's letters teach just one lesson, and one worthy of the Scotsman, <u>Mr. Smith</u>: *a girl must look out for her interest!*"

"And Catherine will look out for hers and marry that milk-blooded coward Linton?"

"Undoubtedly, sir; you see 'tis clear you must either forget the hussy, or—

"Forget her?" I cried. "How can I?"

Juliette smiled at me like an indulgent schoolmaster. "Why, 'tis the simplest thing in the world, sir, and the method can be expressed in a single word—through *vice*. 'Twas long ago amply proven that the simplest way to forget a body is simply to fuck another..." (I started at this piquant language, but Juliette, overtaken by a kind of philosophical paroxysm, continued with a smile) "...Fuck, sir; yes, *fuck and forget*—'tis a motto should be branded on the brow of every mincing, love-sick <u>Werther</u> alive! Ah, Hurlevent, if you would forget your Cathy, you must fuck like a man released from a stay of execution; you must indulge every inclination and fancy, no matter how extreme; you must set yourself to demolishing as many as possible of those fleshy membranes which, in Europe, deluded maidens always confuse with their virtue. For I ask you, sir: when you have ravished twenty different beauties, each prettier than the last, what will little Catherine Earnshaw be to you?"

"Ah, I could not forget Cathy if it were a hundred!"

"In that case," Juliette said with a shrug, "you must simply dispose of your rival. With your fortune, you will return to England a gentleman; nothing could then be simpler than to challenge Linton to a duel, and if he is the craven creature you make him out to be, your victory is assured."

Although my adventures with Dorval had left me no stranger to the use of a pistol, I told Juliette that I could not possibly accept this plan—for I feared it would make Cathy unhappy.

"The moral law to which you allude, my friend," the lady interrupted, "appears altogether meaningless to me, a superstitious illusion; since I was twelve years old I have never admitted the existence of any obligation to repay like with like. On the contrary! We must do precisely as we please; Nature depends on each being's pursuit of his interest, 'tis the simplest thing in the world to demonstrate—"

Some involuntary sign of mine forestalled another philosophical digression. It was her health I feared for, rather than my patience; the Comtesse's flushed face indicated that, the further she entered into her philosophy, she closer she came to actual mania!

"Well, I will skip to the end," Juliette said, cooling herself with a black fan. "I admit the existence of only one law—to enjoy oneself, at no matter whose expense; and this admitted, my friend, the only question is: how will you manage it? Does Linton, for instance, have a sister?"

"Yes, Isabella." I blinked. "Madame, you do not mean to suggest that I should—"

Juliette smiled by way of answer. "Is she even slightly attractive?"

"She'll be eighteen when I return; a girl of that age can hardly help it..." I smiled into my cup of chocolate as I warmed to the idea. "As for her mind, the less said about it the better..."

"Then you run no risk of falling in love with her?"

"Easier to channel a waterfall into a thimble!"

"Excellent; in an intrigue of this kind one must take great care to shun love; it has no place in cold seduction, as the letters of the Vicomte de Valmont and the Marquise de Merteuil so charmingly prove. I knew them both—braver libertines there never were, yet the instant love entered into their hearts, they abandoned their shrewd policies, and lost all! You have read those letters, my friend? Then take Valmont's conduct as your own—alternate severe distance and urgent familiarity; assume moods of profound silence; counterfeit, in a word, that nauseating condition Englishmen call _sensibility_; all this done, an inexperienced girl cannot fail to fall in love with you."

"Can it be so simple?"

"It is, sir—and what's more, the simpler the girl, the easier she'll fall in love, for love is nothing more than a philosophical mistake, and 'tis probable that the progress of Enlightenment shall eventually purge it from Europe!"

"I cannot agree with you, Madame..."

"Hurlevent, my poor friend!" Juliette sighed. "How is it that you cannot see the chains in which you are bound? You'd forfeit a grand life in France for the sake of—"

"A chance at happiness," I replied, adding tartly: "For Madame, if I accept your proposition that one must enjoy oneself at no matter whose expense, I can see no other course!"

"Yet how infinitely simpler to do the opposite!" Juliette cried. A strange fire had lit itself in her beautiful black eyes. "Ah, Hurlevent, your obstinacy drives me to despair... come, abandon love; cast down that false idol, shatter that icon to a thousand pieces, and crown in its place, like a *lingam* of the Orient, the image of that merry god, *Vice*! 'Tis libertine vice we have to thank for every intellectual, every lubricious delight; for all good things on earth, for life itself! Nature spurs us to vice, habit inures us to its ills; in short, *vice makes the world go round*, and all the teachings of scoundrel clerics and imbecile parents will never suppress it...ah, the thought overwhelms me...overheats me... Come, my handsome friend, let's fuck straight away; let's inspect that Lascar's prick of yours, doubtless 'tis circumcised..." Here Juliette actually grabbed me through my breeches, and I will not deny that by now lust had stirred similar thoughts in me.

"Ah, 'tis magnificent!" she exclaimed, quickly locating the object of her search. "Dear Hurlevent, let's pass beyond all limits, let's drink a toast to vice—pledge our very souls to vice—abandon ourselves to—to—"

All at once the lady froze; her arms clutched at shapes not present; sweat stood out on her noble, powdered brow; I feared that she was undergoing an actual fit!

"Madame!" I cried.

"—To virtue, sir, to virtue," she said, in a different tone. "Ah, you will forgive my scattered thoughts, sir; I am prone to these fainting spells—as I was saying, we must bend our hearts to God's Providence, and allow our conduct to be governed by the strictest principles of probity and honor...."

"What! _Virtue_? But Madame la Comtesse was just—"

"Ah, sir, you have mistaken me for my sister; 'tis true we look most similar, but our characters and fortunes could not be more divergent! Her wicked deeds maintain her as a countess, while I am a fugitive, ill-used at every turn; she is rich, I penniless; she has allies in every corner, I am alone against the world...in a word, she is Juliette, while I am merely the unfortunate _Justine_..."

I stared at the lady like a fool.

"But be so good as to remind me, sir, of the errand on which you came..."

I explained my situation again—and now, as "Justine," the very same lady proceeded to give me instructions completely contrary to what she'd said a moment before, recommending courteous reserve, resignation to my fate, prayer, obedience of god's commandments, and complete exile from Wuthering Heights!

"But you grow silent, sir; I hope my words do not displease you..."

"I was only marveling at the idea that <u>two souls might inhabit one body</u>," I replied.

The lady smiled at this. "Ah, sir, but did you not tell me ten minutes ago that ever since you were a boy you've carried Cathy in your heart?"

I left the Château de Lorsagne with my mouth hanging open and my hair falling out of its ribbon, feeling more confused than when I came! My carriage rattled along in the night; in a sour mood, I began to frame my rebuke to Dorval. Yet the more I reflected on my encounter, the more I had to stop myself from laughing, and at last I gave in. The moon outside the shutters was bright, the air bracing; I drew deep breaths of it.

"That rascal Dorval was not so wrong to send me here," I mused. "The vice of Juliette and the virtue of Justine are identical... The same intelligence works at equal strength in each spirit, like a blindfolded runner pointed in one direction, then its opposite...

"Yet love is equally unknown to both, equally beyond virtue and vice! Finding it immune to their arguments and systems, they cast it aside—one to perfect her seductions, the other to avoid being seduced in this world. Very well, to England! If it's love they would deny, it's love's promptings I'll obey—I'll make Cathy feel that love in proportion to my love, suffer in proportion to my suffering—and she'll come back to me, I'm sure, or else I never knew the girl!"

I was arrested a few days afterward, in connection with an earlier robbery, though Dorval assures me he will intercede with the authorities; he fears the report I might make of him! And when he does so, I will quit this land for good. That, sir, that is the story of my interview with Juliette, alias "Justine"—whom I cannot help but judge the most extraordinary lady, or rather *ladies*, in France."

Conclusion

The V Manuscript marks the instant when Sade learned of Juliette and Justine and became fascinated by their history. Scholars now believe that after his release from the Château de Vincennes he sought out Juliette-Justine with the intentions of ghost-writing her autobiography(-ies). (These works, in 1801, would earn Sade another prison sentence and the moral ire of Napoleon Bonaparte himself.) For full discussion of Sade's decision to split Juliette and Justine's personalities into separate biographies, see 2012 Justine/Juliette Controversy.

While the discovery of the V Manuscript revolutionized Wuthering Heights studies less than it did Sade studies, scholars agree[citation needed] that it confirms the explanation of Heathcliff's three missing years first outlined by Yeats.

Literary theorist Ward Dreamday has also controversially claimed that the V Manuscript may be an early source for Friedrich Nietzsche's remark that "What is done out of love always takes place beyond good and evil."[7]

Notes/References

1   Charles Percy Sanger. *The Structure of Wuthering Heights.* [Hogarth Essays, XIX], London: Hogarth Press, 1926.

2   Brontë, Emily: *Wuthering Heights* (Oxford World's Classics, 1998) p. 3.

3   William Butler Yeats. *The Fortunes of Heathcliff in France.* [Occasional Papers of The Yorkshire Ghost-hunters' Fraternity.] Leeds: Pilcrow House, 1927.

4   *The Proceedings of the Old Bailey, 11ᵗʰ July 1781. The TRIAL of FRANCIS HENRY DE LA MOTTE, for High Treason.* [Available at http://www.oldbaileyonline.org/]

5   London Lantern, *A Witness's Account of the Trial of One Gimmerton.* 21st June 1781.

6   Ward Dreamday. "A Boy Must Look Out For His Interest: Sade Contra Smith, Nietzsche Contra Brontë, Sedgwick Contra Winnicott." [*New Historicist Review*, v.14] University of Chicago Press, December 2012.

7   Ibid.

See Also

- The Coherence of Gothic Conventions – Eve Kosofsky Sedgwick's doctoral thesis
- Dialectic of Enlightenment
- Disassociative Identity Disorder
- French Literature of the Eighteenth Century
- Gothic Novels
- Transitional Object – psychoanalytic critics such as Dreamday read Heathcliff's link with Catherine as an instance of the transitional phenomena described by D.W. Winnicott.

Madeline Usher Usher

Alisa Alering

Madeline Usher Usher

Madeline Usher Usher (14 August, 1801 — c. November, 1837) was a popular and prolific poet of the <u>Victorian era</u>, notable for regularly published volumes of verse that were praised for both their "refined pathos" and "fresh strange music."[1] Despite falling into disfavor in the latter half of the nineteenth century, Usher Usher was "rediscovered" in the 1950s, and has since come to be considered one of the most significant poets of her era.[1] Afflicted since childhood by an undiagnosed illness that resulted in severe head and spinal pain, wasting, and increasing periods of incapacitating paralysis, a dramatic account first published in the United States in 1839[2] reported that Madeline had finally succumbed to her disease at the age of thirty-six. Modern excavations at the site of the family estate uncovered the final volumes of Madeline's diary, which, together with the re-examination of correspondence between Madeline and her contemporaries, suggested that the death of the celebrated poet may have been caused by a pathologically devoted admirer.[3]

CONTENTS

Life and Career

Family Background

Madeline was born into an ancient family that traced its origins back to an English yeoman who, in 1173, was granted 40 hectares of farm and woodland for an unnamed service to Henry II, possibly for military service in Ireland.[4] Though without noble title, the Ushers took pride in their ancient and unbroken heritage, handing down their name along with their growing fortune. Proving themselves able farmers and businessmen, the Ushers soon acquired great wealth. Inheritance was often dependent upon the condition that the name Usher be used by the beneficiary. Given the strong tradition, Madeline used "Madeline Usher Watson Usher" on legal documents and often signed herself as "Madeline Usher Usher" in personal correspondence, though she dropped the second instance of her surname in her published works.[4]

William, head of the Usher family in the late seventeenth century, substantially increased the family's wealth by investing in the West Indian colonies, primarily Jamaica. When Madeline's father, Jasper, became head of the family in 1785, the Usher holdings in the Caribbean (five ships, two sugar plantations, a refining mill, and an estimated 300 slaves) outstripped the value of their property in their native England.[4]

Financial disaster fell upon the Ushers in 1803, two years after Madeline's birth, when an unusually fierce storm season struck Jamaica, destroying two of the Usher's trans-Atlantic cargo vessels and causing thousands of pounds worth of damage to the sugar cane crop.[4] One of the plantations, Rose Hall, was sold to cover the losses, but the family never regained the fortune of their earlier days.

Interestingly, Madeline penned an early poem decrying the abuses of slavery, titled "The Footsteps of Fear."[5] She supported the abolitionist cause all her life, despite the fact that abolition would entail deeper losses for the family's already declining fortunes.[citation needed]

Her family's responsibility in the slave trade weighed upon her conscience. As she wrote to Maria Rackrent in 1827, "I belong to a family of West Indian slaveholders, and if I believed in curses, I should be afraid."[6]

Childhood

Madeline Usher Watson Usher was born on 14 August 1801, in Usher Hall, in the remote village of Usher, England. She was the first surviving child born to her parents, Jasper Usher Watson Usher and Sarah Pope Russell. An older sister, Annabelle, had been born in 1799, but died three weeks after birth. Though the famous account of the dissolution of the Usher empire represents Madeline and her brother Roderick as twins,[2] she was in fact two years his elder, Roderick being born in September 1803.[4] A letter to a mutual acquaintance from the family solicitor, who visited the Usher estate in early 1835, remarked on how the siblings had grown to resemble one another: "They have lived alone together for such a number of years, seeing no one but their few servants, that they have grown as alike in appearance as a husband and wife long-married."[4] A third son, Lawrence, was born three years after Roderick, in March 1806. Madeline's mother endured an unusually long labor giving birth to Lawrence, and died shortly afterwards of puerperal sepsis.[3] Sarah Usher was laid to rest in the family burial-ground, a remote knoll some distance from the house on the Usher estate.[4]

The spring of 1808 was bitterly cold, and an epidemic of scarlet fever ravaged the village, afflicting all three Usher children. Two-year-old Lawrence died, and while both Madeline and Roderick recovered, Roderick developed rheumatic fever as a complication of the streptococcal infection.[citation needed] Roderick's heart was weakened by his battle with the fever. Coupled with periodic recurrences of fever, his father decreed that Roderick was to be educated at home for several additional years before being sent to school in Bristol. Madeline was permitted to attend lessons with her brother's tutor throughout this time, giving her access to an education that was unusually rigorous for a girl of her time.[3]

Madeline's first poem, "Stanzas On the Contemplation of Distant Lands," was written at the age of nine.[5] Her father enclosed a copy with a letter to Madeline's aunt, his sister, Mary Usher Boyd, who lived abroad at the time, her husband being engaged on a trade mission in <u>Amsterdam</u>. The original manuscript is held in the Valdemar Collection at the <u>Metzengerstein Library</u> in the <u>Netherlands</u>.[5]

Illness

Shortly after Roderick finally departed for school in 1815, Madeline suffered the first attack of the mysterious illness that was to plague her for the rest of her life. On a warm day in late August,[4] intending to visit her mother's grave, Madeline ventured onto the causeway that connected the Usher house with the countryside beyond the tarn, whereupon she was struck with a "searing pain"[1] to the temples. She dropped her basket, the flowers and supplies she carried for cleaning the tomb spilling about her feet. As the pain subsided, she stooped to retrieve the items but found she had no control of her feet or her arms or any part of her body. She tried to cry out for help, but could make no sound. She later described this incident as "when I first knew terror."[7]

The attack was accompanied by a sort of "interior vision"[4] that Madeline described as being "enveloped in an endless white tunnel, the walls smooth and uniform, without interruption or device. The walls were lit, but diffusely, without any obvious source of light. The extreme whiteness suggested the heavenly realms, and yet I always had the greatest sensation of heaviness bearing down upon me, as if I were contained at an exceeding depth below the earth."[7]

She was noticed in her frozen attitude by a groom, who alerted Madeline's father. Together, the men carried the rigid girl into the house where, as they passed under the <u>Gothic</u> archway of the hall, she suddenly regained the strength of her limbs.

Further episodes followed throughout her life. Sometimes the pain afflicted her head, at other times her neck, spine, and legs. She counted it as one of the most significant episodes of her life. "Despite the terror, I felt as if in some way I had been freed. What did it matter if I could not go to school like my brother? What did it matter that I could not travel to see the world from which all the goods and comforts of my home derived? I had a sense of my existence as eternal—I was trapped, and yet I would always be still inside myself. All of the world should come to me."[7]

Literary Success

Shortly after this first attack, Madeline began to write poetry with a new vigor, and of a markedly different nature from her juvenile efforts. She continued to utilize the traditional forms of romance and sonnet, but that "fresh, strange music" with which she is identified, now came strongly to the fore.[citation needed]

Her first effort in this new vein, "Athens, On the Eve of War," was published in the *The New Monthly Companion* in 1817. The editor, <u>Charles Blackwood</u>, was so impressed with his new contributor that he wrote to ask if she had more work. He became a lifelong supporter and friend, publishing many of her poems, as well as the essay, "The Maid's Garden," in the *Companion*.[5]

Usher Usher's first collection, *The Sphinx, and Other Poems*, was published in 1820.[1,5] It strongly shows the influence of her Classical education, as well as an "exquisite"[8] appreciation of the natural world. This was followed by a translation of the tale of <u>Helen</u>, from <u>Euripides</u>, in 1821. It wasn't until 1824, with the publication of "<u>*The Romaunt of Blanche*</u>," that Madeline attracted wider attention.[5] Published to great acclaim by <u>Weedon & Howe</u>, *Blanche* garnered a letter of praise from <u>William Wordsworth</u>.[4]

Though frail in appearance, with a "slight, delicate figure" and "large, liquid eyes,"[3] Madeline was largely free of her illness during this time, suffering only occasional pains and muscle weakness, without a recurrence of full body paralysis, which allowed her to travel to London for the first and only time in her life. Through her aunt, Mary Boyd, a patron of the arts now returned from the Continent and living in the artistic neighborhood of <u>Belgravia</u>, Madeline was introduced to literary figures of the day, including <u>Samuel Taylor Coleridge</u>, <u>Thomas Lovell Beddoes</u>, and <u>Maria Rackrent</u>, who became a lifelong friend and confidante to the isolated Madeline.

Upon returning from London, Madeline was struck with a severe cataleptic attack,[7] and from that point on, the attacks became more frequent, sometimes afflicting her more than once in a single day, or leaving her paralyzed for hours at a time. On one occasion,[4] she was struck dumb and carried into her room by the servants, where she lay on her bed unmoving from mid-day until dawn the next morning. She became reclusive in her habits, sticking close to the house and rarely venturing beyond the grounds of the Usher estate, out of fear that "I should be struck dumb like a monument on the village green."[6]

She compensated for the narrowing of her physical world by traveling greater distances in her imagination. She began work on the *Poems of Castile* (1826), a collection that conjures an exotic medieval realm of chivalry, kings, and fantastic beasts.[5]

Severe financial losses in the family's Jamaican holdings in the autumn of 1826 sent Jasper Usher into a decline. He suffered a stroke and died within a month of receiving the news.[1] Roderick became the head of the family, a role for which, it soon became clear, he was temperamentally unsuited.

Madeline's grief over the loss of her father combined with a worsening of her illness suggest that for a while she came to rely heavily upon <u>laudanum</u>, <u>morphine</u>, and other painkillers, which may account for the five-year gap between publication of *Poems of Castile* (1826) and *The Courtship of Lady Margret* (1831).[7]

Sherard Underwood

Upon publication of *The Courtship of Lady Margret* (1831), Usher Usher received letters of congratulation from literary acquaintances such as Charles Blackwood, <u>Alfred Lord Tennyson</u>, and <u>Edgar Allan Poe</u>.[9] In a letter to Maria Rackrent, Usher reported an equal increase in correspondence from the general public. This fan mail offered praise for her work and compliments to her person — one appreciative gentleman went so far as to propose marriage, writing, presumably as an incentive, that he was possessed of "a six-room house in <u>Norfolk</u>, somewhat damp but in a pleasant situation."[3] Madeline replied to many of these notes in her own hand, thanking her readers for their "generous praise" and "kind thoughts."[3]

It is in this period that Usher Usher's troubled relationship with her future murderer [flagged — unsubstantiated] began. In a letter of 26 February 1832, Usher Usher writes to Maria Rackrent that she has received several missives from "a peculiar personage, calling himself <u>Sherard Underwood</u>, who has been most persistent in his messages."[6]

Several months later, Usher Usher wrote to Charles Blackwood, editor of *The New Monthly Companion,* enclosing a copy of a poem that had been sent to her by Underwood. "I am not unaware of the honor in being the first to look upon a poet's newborn offering, but in this case I confess that something lies between its lines which disturbs and offends me." She continues, saying she feared that the verse revealed "a nature quite unwell, and fascinated with all that is morbid."[10] Regrettably, the poem itself has been lost.

In subsequent years, Underwood persisted in his correspondence, showering Usher Usher with his letters, affections, and poetical effusions. In 1832, shortly after the first edition of *Sonnets* appeared, Madeline complained to Maria Rackrent of the volume of literary offerings that Underwood continued to lay at her feet: "That one man should contain so many words! He presses upon me reams of his work, pages and papers and sheaves until, if I kept them all, I should be buried under them, suffocated by his sentences, entombed in his daydreams. Considering the quantity of language he requires to communicate the fascinations of his soul, it is a wonder that a single word remains in the English tongue for the use of another person."[6]

Though Madeline insisted to Rackrent that she "in no way"[6] had encouraged Underwood's attentions, he responded to the 1836 publication of *Aurora: A Celebration of Love*—an allegorical romance set in the imaginary kingdom of Lofoden[5]—as Usher Usher's public proclamation of the romantic "understanding" that he felt existed between them.[10]

The Visit

Sherard Underwood arrived in the village of Usher in September 1837,[11] apparently provoked by the publication of *Aurora* to meet in person the idolized object of his affections. Madeline wrote to Maria Rackrent of their uninvited guest: "He arrived on our doorstep on the most dismal night, claiming acquaintance with my brother from their schooldays. Roderick greeted him affably, but I think, given his condition of late, that he should greet Ozymandias himself with just the same limp handshake and vague air. My brother has not been well since Father's death—so ill-suited is he to bear the weight of our ailing family. If he would only let me aid him...but he will not hear of it."[6]

Madeline suffered Underwood's presence for the sake of her brother. Two weeks after his arrival, she wrote to Maria: "My brother has been low and without cheer for some time, and is now very glad to have a friend. Mr. Underwood has disposed himself to be very charming to Roderick, sitting up nights with him, admiring his paintings, and applauding his compositions upon the guitar. To see him even half way returned to the lively brother of my youth is worth any amount of inconvenience to myself."[6]

Not long after, her letters to Rackrent cease, and it was not until Madeline's diaries were recovered some 100 years later that any information on the months leading up to her death became available. The reason for this is suggested by her diary entry of 10 October 1837, in which she writes of her fears that Underwood is "intercepting my correspondence and reading my letters. He is like some awful spirit who has invaded our home; this ancient refuge of the Ushers that has withstood armies, is now broken, besieged from the inside by this petty tyrant with his insistent manner and his ten-shilling shoes."[11]

In late October, she complained of the "flurry" of works that Underwood presented to her seeking praise. "Today he brought me, as a sort of gift, his 'romance', a dragon-slaying fantasy whose hero 'Ethelred' is very mighty indeed, banging down doors and quaffing enormous quantities of wine. It is clever enough, I suppose, but he has none of that genuine spark of the true artist, consumed as he is by visions of his own glory."[11]

Though Madeline initially welcomed Underwood's friendship with Roderick, she now accused him of encouraging her brother in a "sort of aesthetic insanity,"[11] playing music at all hours of the day and night. "He [Underwood] haunts the piano, pounding out a tilting, reeling wild <u>waltz</u> that jigs and drags me off-balance until I feel I would jump in the tarn just to have the chill black waters close quietly over my head."[11]

In her entry for 5 November 1837, she reported that earlier that evening while her brother was engaged in a fit of furious painting, Underwood paid a visit to her chambers. She writes: "He came to tell me that not only does he love me, but that he knows that I love him. When I denied it, he would not hear my words of protest, but said with infuriating patience that he understood and shared my desire to hide our love in public, but I need not dissemble when we were alone. I demurred, and he said that he knew the proof of my love. From my shelves he removed a volume of *Aurora* and preceded to read out several lines, dictating their meaning to me, with a superior smile. As if he should know the private thoughts of my mind better than I! Fool that I was, I attempted reason, explicating the intent of my craft, how Aurora was not myself, but an <u>allegory</u>. At this he reared back as if insulted. He grew very white in the face, and he spat out that I should 'take care' not to push him too far. That, 'though his love for me made him forgiving, he could excuse my willfulness only so far.' Oh, that I should ever have lifted a pen, to be pierced and tormented by weapons forged from my own words, now turned against me."[11]

Secret Marriage

It has been proposed by some[3] that Underwood and Usher Usher were married, at his insistence, at some point during his enforced stay on the Usher estate. Skeptics point to the diaries, which make no mention of a marriage ceremony, nor to any increase in intimacy between Usher and Underwood. Supporters of the theory[3] maintain that the offense of the forced marriage was too great for a personality as sensitive as Madeline's, and that as a poet she knew the permanency of the written word, and so would not admit to such an offensive event, even in a space as private as a diary. Scholars have pointed to one of the last entries in the diary, claiming it as a coded reference to a horror Madeline could not bring herself to record openly.

"It is done. It is done. My heart shall break. Would not death, the cold ground of the distant hillside, be a better, more welcome fate than this? [...Illegible...] I vow this now—when my time comes I will haunt this man who has yoked himself to me like the hooks of a Spanish needle. I will pursue him and hound him unto his very last days, which I will make every much a misery as he has mine."[3,11]

Much of this is difficult to confirm, as in 1835 the Usher estate was destroyed by a catastrophic fire, in which both Madeline and Roderick were believed to have perished.[1] Underwood escaped unharmed, turning up at the Devon Arms, a public house and hostelry some forty miles distant. Questioned by the magistrate, he claimed to have no knowledge of the fire or its causes, having departed from Usher early the previous morning.[10]

The deaths of Madeline and Roderick, and the destruction of the Usher house, remained at first a local affair, known only in the immediate region. However, in 1839, a melodramatic account of Roderick's insanity, Madeline's burial alive, and the avalanche that consumed the house, appeared in the <u>United States</u>, published in a <u>Baltimore</u> magazine by an "unknown" author, using the <u>pseudonym</u>, "<u>A.E. Poe</u>."[4] This sensational account drew great attention on both sides of the Atlantic, resulting in even greater fame and demand for Madeline's works.

Publishing Success

The sensation surrounding Usher Usher's death may have contributed to the success of a large collection of her previously unpublished poems (*Women & Men*, 1840)[5] that were discovered after her death and brought out posthumously by Weedon & Howe, her London publishers, setting contemporary records for number of copies sold. The edition was edited by Sherard Underwood, who claimed that Madeline had been at work on these poems in secret until just a few days before her death. In the foreword to the first edition, Underwood relates that the poems had come into his possession, and were therefore spared from destruction by fire, because Madeline had experienced a vision during one of her cataleptic fits, and had afterwards begged him to take the manuscripts with him to a place of safety. He pleaded with her to allow him to stay and protect her, but she had her brother order him from their home,[12] presumably for Underwood's own safety. None of this, however, explains why he did not present the poems to Weedon & Howe until after the "The Fall of the House of Usher" piece appeared in Baltimore, several years after Madeline's death.

Discovery of the Diaries

Fourteen volumes of Madeline's diaries were discovered locked in a strongbox, in a vault beneath the oldest part of the house—the original feudal keep—when the ruins of the estate were excavated in 1997, prior to the development of a <u>luxury hotel</u> on the site.[3] The walls and floors of the storage vault were sheathed in <u>copper</u> and protected by a massive iron door, which shielded the diaries from the fire that destroyed the rest of the house, almost as if Madeline had some knowledge of the coming conflagration. [citation needed] The diaries begin in 1810, when Madeline was eight years old, and present a complete record of her life, missing only the volumes for 1817-1818 and March 1828–October 1828.[11] The discovery of the diaries has been a boon to scholars studying her body of work, offering insights as to her inspiration and filling in gaps in her biography.[3]

Some scholars, however, cast doubt on the evidence presented via the latter volumes of Madeline's diaries.[7] Since the first attack of her illness at the age of 13, Madeline was almost certainly a regular user of opiates such as laudanum and morphine,[7] which were commonly prescribed at the time. It is generally accepted[citation needed] among literary scholars that the effects of these drugs almost certainly contributed to the vividness of her poetic imagination. Camilla Gliddon, professor of Comparative Literature at the University of West Anglia, has suggested that after 25 years of increasing dependence on opiates, the final "paranoid" entries into Madeline's diary can hardly be taken as the literal truth.[13]

Works (Collections)

1820: *The Sphinx, and Other Poems.* Privately printed.

1821: *Helen,* translated from the Greek of Euripides, and Other Poems. London: Weedon & Howe

1824: *The Romaunt of Blanche.* London: Weedon & Howe

1826: *Poems of Castile.* London: Weedon & Howe

1831: *Lady Margret's Courtship*. London: Weedon & Howe; New York: R.R. Ellison & Co.

1834: *Sonnets*. London: Weedon & Howe;

1836: *Aurora: A Celebration of Love*. London: Weedon & Howe

1837: *Sonnets*, ("New Edition"). London: Weedon & Howe; New York: R.R. Ellison & Co.

1840: Women and Men (posthumous). London: Weedon & Howe; New York: Wiley & Putnam

Notes/References

1   Pamela Roget, "Usher Usher, Madeline (1801-1837)", *Oxford Dictionary of National Biography*, Oxford University Press, 2004; online edition, October 2008.

2   Poe, A. E. [Pseud.] "The Fall of the House of Usher," *Burton's Gentleman's Magazine*, Vol. V, September 1839.

3   Booth-Khan, Marie. *Madeline Usher Usher: A New Look*. Chicago University Press, 2005.

4   Hobson, Rose. *The Life of Madeline Usher Usher*. Cambridge University Press, 1932.

5   Johnson, Eleanora & Thomas A. Hawk, Eds. *The Works of Madeline Usher Usher*. London, New York: Penguin, 1982, 3rd revised ed.

6   Snook, Peter, ed. *The Letters of Madeline Usher Usher to Maria Rackrent, 1825-1837*. Chicago University Press, 1965. New edition, 2001.

7   *Inspiration or Affliction: The Visions of Madeline Usher Usher*. London: Virago, 2003.

8   Bedloe, A.R. "Introduction." *The Sphinx, and Other Poems*. [critical ed.] New York: Macmillan, 1965.

9   Klimm, Nicholas. "Introduction." *The Courtship of Lady Margret*. London, New York: Penguin, 1990.

10 Ripley, Alexa. *Forger, Fraud, Murderer: The Life and Crimes of Sherard Underwood*. Modern Library, 2006.

11 W.M. Wilson & Jenna Ponto, eds. *"All The World Should Come To Me": The Complete Diaries of Madeline Usher Usher*. Cambridge University Press, 1999.

12 Underwood, Sherard. "Introduction." *Women and Men*. London: Weedon & Howe, 1839.

13 Gliddon, Camilla. *Poisoners, Prisoners and Pariahs: Literature and Criminal Psychology*. Oklahoma University Press, 2008.

Maisie and Amomma

Mark Rich

Maisie and Amomma

An English painter, Maisie exhibited from the late 1880s to early 1900s in England and France. Her *Melancolia* series attracted some notoriety late in her life, although the works themselves went missing after her death in 1909.

Amomma was Maisie's childhood short-hair goat.

Maisie

Maisie's association with artist <u>Richard Heldar</u>, whose story appears in Kipling's 1890 novel *The Light That Failed*, began early. She and Dick grew up as foster children of a Mrs. Jennett, who lived near Fork Keeling on the English Channel. From Dick's point of view their lives echoed lines by <u>Edgar Alan Poe</u>: "*I* was a child and *she* was a child,/ In this kingdom by the sea." Just after professing their childhood love to one another, Dick's and Maisie's paths veered apart for ten years. By the time they met again, Heldar had suffered a head-wound as a war correspondent in North Africa — and his military prints and paintings had come into vogue in London. Maisie in the interim had also turned to painting. She had lost the love she felt as a child, however — if indeed she ever felt the same emotion "Dicky" did; and in adulthood her feelings toward him remained consistently friendly if lacking in romantic fervor. After Heldar's war wound caught up with him and left him blind, Maisie thought she might find it in her heart to rescue him from his new, deep isolation—and briefly left off her painting efforts, in France, to see him. This last reunion went poorly, however; and she went back to her artwork—the first of her imaginary portraits of *Melancolia*. Heldar's failure in wooing Maisie came as a blow to him. Even during his ten years away she had held a central place in his heart.[1]

Kipling knew more about Maisie than his novel reveals. It does offer clues, however. Near its midpoint, Dick Heldar speaks of having done one painting that fully expressed his talents—which he based on lines from Poe's "Annabel Lee": "And neither the angels in Heaven above,/ Nor the demons down under the sea,/ Can ever dissever my soul from the soul/ Of the beautiful Annabel Lee."[2] In these lines Heldar recognizes his situation, albeit subconsciously. He is tied inextricably to Maisie.

Kipling withheld Maisie's full name to avoid embarrassing a woman then still alive. Maisie had a *matronym*—for her mother had dwelled in a tomb by the sea, when gravid—or "gravèd," as the popular press would have it. Maisie was one of the *somnifils* that Victorian society regarded with some alarm; for they were appearing in uncomfortably high numbers in the later 1800s.

Although he was writing a bit late to have played the role of father to Maisie, Scottish poet <u>James Thomson, "B.V.,"</u> has been considered a possible candidate because of his lines: "The Lady of the images: supine,/ Deathstill, lifesweet, with folded palms she lay:/ And kneeling there as at a sacred shrine/ A young man wan and worn who seemed to pray"—before her "uncorrupted face."[3] Whether it was Thomson or another, the father expressed his love for his *ideal* at her death-bed: he saw there—or on bier or in casket—his "uncorrupted" Love. Poe's Annabel Lee had become by this time the *Pure Ideal* of all postmortem *ideals*, so that *all* deceased feminine objects of unnatural passion were "Annabel Lee," by type and by name; and all offspring of such unnatural unions bore the matronymic surname Lee—at least in England and France, where Poe's reputation long held a secure place.[4]

This situation failed to arise in America, where Poe's reputation remained somewhat besmirched. Rufus Griswold's unfortunate portrayals had the effect of emotionally inhibiting young American writers and artists when making visits to tombs in search of *ideals*.[5]

Somnifils in England were often called *dreamlings*, because of the then-common poetic practice of describing death in terms of sleep or dream. They went by another name as well. Since "kip" refers to a bed or to sleep, the *somnifils* in some English papers came to be called *kiplings*.

By the later 1860s and '70s, especially in the south of England, church groups kept vigils at newly-closed vaults in case unnatural children should appear and require removal to an orphanage or foster family.[6] The practice of keeping vigils dropped off during the later 1880s and '90s, kipling birthrates having dropped steadily as techno-industrial society, making ever-greater strides in Western Europe, created conditions that discouraged budding artistic souls from adopting the late-Romantic posture necessary in conceiving *somnifils*. Poets still could appreciate the dark soulnight of Modern existence, as depicted in Thomson's poem *The City of Dreadful Night*. No longer, however, could they so easily express such profoundly melancholic thoughts about the dead past.[7] The tomb had become an awkward spot for romance, however unnatural the feelings involved.

The City of Dreadful Night, while far from a holy text for the secular revolution of the later 1800s, was a telling document that exposed the bleak side of the intellectual transformation undertaking England and other Western countries. It presented a depressive Hell of Rationalism, where a deity named Melancolia reigned. Dick Heldar's was typical of later nineteenth-century reactions, in answering the possibility of such a hell by embracing his religion of Art. Maisie in contrast embraced Thomson's response, and became Melancolia herself, even though she had artistic ambitions herself. "I've been beating my wings long enough," she says to Heldar, in speaking of a high honor that might come her way—unconsciously invoking Thomson's image of the winged but flightless Melancolia.[8]

In our day when *somnifils* are uncommon to the point of nonexistence, some confusion has arisen about whether, in Victorian times, the father needed to play a physical role in conception. Since *ideals* give post-entombment birth solely to *somnifils* and never to normal, physically engendered children, *unnatural passion* alone did, indeed, prove sufficient to the task. An *absence* of physical interaction, in fact, may have heightened passion to the requisite level.[9]

This had important ramifications. As the Victorians knew, mothers of *somnifils* were nearly always virgin, thanks to childhood tuberculosis rates.[10] This prompted, in the 1870s and '80s, English churches to urge forward techno-industrial progress with all haste and at all cost—which helps explain why church publications of the time attacked factory conditions in London, Manchester, and elsewhere in so muted a manner, if at all. Not only did pastors and priests hope to win munificent tithings from the burgeoning industrial-manufacturing class; they hoped, too, to obliterate the last remnants of a decadent Romantic Spirit in English society.[11]

The ever-more adulterated *religious* value of "virgin birth" caused the Catholics especial difficulty, in these years, and made them, indeed, industrious in quashing cultural conditions that encouraged *somnifils*. Although Anglican bishops felt less moved by doctrinal considerations, in 1893 they opted to support their Roman church counterparts in proselytizing for industrial progress. By the 1900s demonstrations of late-Romantic sentiments were at low ebb. The churches diverted any lingering effusions, such as the Arts Nouveau and William Morris movements, and steered creative souls in the Futurist and even Dadaist directions latent in the arts since the 1860s. World War I marked the success of this ecumenical campaign. The late-Romantic expression of ultimate Individualism that gave rise to *kiplings* essentially ended with the advent of "world" hostilities.[12]

Although unusual in her artistic ambition, Maisie Lee was a typical dreamling. After her difficult youth she realized her innate potentials were limited due to her being half-child of living man and non-living woman: for she possessed less than half a heart. She felt alone in a desolate internal landscape—a natural feeling, since the *somnifils* support groups, the Leeward Societies of Liverpool and Glasgow, were shut down in London; and she became yet another fey "lady of images." Unable to embrace a more emotional goal in her life, she made artistic fame her sole aim. She signed her works only "Maisie," not realizing that a later generation would have been drawn like moths to flame had they found the "Lee" name among artists of the period.[13]

Amomma

When Mrs. Jennett became guardian to a second orphan, Maisie, her first foster child, Dick Heldar, regarded the girl as "a companion in bondage...who moved about the house silently and for the first few weeks spoke only to the goat that was her chiefest friend on earth and lived in the back-garden. Mrs. Jennett objected to the goat on the grounds that he was unchristian,—which he certainly was."[14] As to the goat, Maisie tells Mrs. Jennett, "Amomma is mine, mine, mine!" Much later she speaks of her art to Dick in the same terms: "It must be my work. Mine,—mine,—mine!"[15] Despite the creature's similarity of name to "Momma," Amomma is a billygoat to whom "nothing is sacred."[16] At the one point when Kipling offers Amomma's thoughts to the reader, it becomes clear that the animal, rather than feeling *owned*, feels he *owns* Dick and Maisie. They are "his property."[17]

Goats were commonplace in Victorian England as elsewhere, with most expressing their common-garden-goat natures in typical animal ways. Others, however, gave evidence of a different aspect to their beings. The connection between *somnifils* and goats was natural and commonplace, due to the inherited insufficiency of romantic feeling on the one part, and the celebrated surfeit on the other. The symbolic death of Pan insured that "the horn of plenty" was available in plentiful supply to his ancestors, since only they, and not the general public, accepted his peculiar patrimony after it had been rendered somewhat unfashionable and was shoved under the rug by Christian society. In childhood, as a consequence, Maisie lived life as a fairly complete child—because she had her perfect complement and counterpart in her constant companion, Amomma.

Ending the first chapter—which is Amomma's only chapter, in Kipling's book—a condensed version, or vision, of what is to come appears: for in the night after Dick and Maisie have revealed and pledged their childhood love to one another, Dick—

> dreamed a wild dream. He had won all the world and brought it to Maisie in a cartridge-box, but she turned it over with her foot, and instead of saying, "Thank you," cried—

> "Where is the brass collar you promised for Amomma? Oh, how selfish you are!"[18]

When Maisie and Dick finally meet again, his first question to her is about Amomma. She replies that the billy-goat died—of overeating. Although she says the cause was not cartridges, the only scene the reader sees of Amomma's probably eclectic eating habits involves his literally eating explosives.[19]

The Red-Haired Girl

In her adult life Maisie shared rooms and studio with another painter Kipling referred to only as "the red-haired girl." Maisie first describes her to Dick as "an impressionist, and all our notions clash."[20] Oddly, in the novel, she often stands *behind* others—as though to butt them from behind, perhaps—or to perform a spirit function, speaking from behind not only Maisie but also Dick—as though speaking *from within*.

In Kipling's novel, this red-headed mystery is emotional and feels for Heldar all the love that Maisie does not. Dick Heldar knows naught of this save through a love-note that, true to form, the red-headed girl sends without signing her name—if ever she did, in fact, have a name. Dick never gave or sent the red-haired girl anything—being blind in this way even before rendered sightless.

Rudyard Kipling

Rudyard Kipling, born in Bombay, began publishing in India where his stories enjoyed early popularity. By the time his world travels of 1887-89 ended in London, new English publications of his work were meeting with great success. Interest in the young writer had appeared so immediately and grew so rapidly, however, for other than purely literary reasons. Efforts both in support of and in suppression of *kiplings* fascinated the English public. That a writer should appear as a Kipling caused a sensation. Some regarded it as Byronic posturing; others, as blackly heathen. Kipling found himself with a strange fame—after having appeared on the English literary scene with exquisite ill-timing, considering his name.

That he was *not* an actual kipling came in for little question. He was not Rudyard *Lee*. Even so the *somnifil* association made him a subject of wide discussion: his was already a household name. "Kipling," of course, was his patronym. However awkwardly, it had helped raise his stories into public view—leaving him unable to throw it aside.

Writing his first novel in these awkward days, Kipling opted to balance a largely factual narrative with a subtext expressing his fears that he, together with his artistic triumphs, would end up sacrificed to the increasingly industrialized society that was consistently friendly but that would not and could not love him in return. He adroitly exploited the energies surrounding dreamlings without mentioning them, except in his byline. He evoked them through suggestion, however, in the characters of Maisie and her imaginary alter-ego, Melancolia.[20-B]

Perhaps due to this over-subtlety, the novel failed to catch on.

The Paintings

Kipling published his novel before Maisie won even the minor notice she later would; and, as a consequence, the reader never learns that Maisie's preoccupation with Melancolia before Heldar's death became fixation afterwards. She painted no other subject. Although these late paintings appeared in galleries, documenting them has proven difficult since contemporary reviews often failed to name works or artists.[21] Confusing matters is the sheer number of *Melancolia*s exhibited in London and Paris in the last quarter of the nineteenth century. Maisie by herself produced dozens of works under that title, gradually depicting an ever-stranger figure of winged dispiritude—with the woman's face based on no known model: for her Melancolia appeared increasingly whiskered and horned like a goat—qualities that won Maisie her small share of notoriety.[22]

Some regard it as significant that upon Amomma's death, an inversion of the billygoat had appeared in Maisie's life. As Etta Pines-Sawyer writes, this inversion-figure "under-eats, not over-eats; she is feminine and not masculine; she is passionately possessed by Heldar rather than possessing him. She is red-haired as if to evoke the chimera's breath of fire—for she is illusory, vanishing and reappearing at will. So is this anonymous anomaly indeed Maisie's soul-priest Ammoma, her *anima*-animal, her unchristian *imam*?"[23]

The nameless red-haired girl also painted *Melancolia*s in her last years, basing these works on ten years of Maisie sketches. A series exhibited in London in the 1890s illustrating moments from *Dreadful Night* seems hers, as well.[24] Gallery records list them as by *Anon*.

Notes/References

1   Heldar's friend Torpenhow, the famous news correspondent, has made this clear. *See* "Names Mentioned During Heldar's Deliriums: Torpenhow Remembers." *Times*. April 3, 1889, p. 30.

2   Kipling, Rudyard. *The Light That Failed*. Albatross Library:
    New York. Undated, p. 108.

3   Thomson, James. *The City of Dreadful Night*. Canongate
    Classics: Edinburgh. 1993, pp. 48-9. *See also* Pines, Georgina
    Meredith. "Unsuccessful in Love — or Successful? James
    Thomson and the Female of the Poetic Species." *Transactions,
    Bowmore Literary Society*. Thomson Society West: Glasgow.
    1923.

4   Angolia, Mel. "Acceptable Names for Unacceptable Children."
    In Adelbert, Frebert, ed., *Children, and Other Victorian
    Embarrassments*. Parenting Press: Hackensack. 1976, pp.
    267-72.

5   Poe's model for "Annabel Lee" was, in fact, a married woman;
    and his poem was a work of art more than a personal
    statement. English and Continental poets and artists,
    ignorant of this, took Poe literally and discovered what he
    never did — the potency of unnatural passion with regards to
    ideals.

6   Here the Leeward Societies had their beginnings. Their
    French counterparts gave their name to Émile Zola's last
    novel, *Les Somneliers, ou, Les Chats Noirs*, about a group
    of *sommeliers* who discover a crypt full of *somnifils* when
    opening a newly and suspiciously bricked-in section of
    a wine cellar. The publisher unfortunately burned the
    manuscript, saying the novel would attract attention and
    make Zola "too popular."

7   Instead, the *not-yet-alive future* increasingly became the
    source of unnatural children — a subject outside the purview
    of this entry. These later unnatural children were such
    materialistic manifestations they excited few Victorian
    qualms. Unlike the melancholic *somnifils*, they were difficult
    to distinguish from the *purely physically engendered* children
    then being ushered into life in extraordinary numbers.

8   Kipling, op. cit., p. 54. Maisie is moved to adopt this subject
    when her studiomate reads from Thomson about Melancolia:

p. 123. The verse from Section XXI of *Dreadful Night*, which begins with the line "Baffled and beaten back she works on still," does capture Maisie's character — as the roommate realizes. It offers an apt portrait of someone operating with *insufficient heart*.

9   Hibberling, Lisa. "Easings of Social Strictures in Victorian Tombs." *Kipling Studies*. March 1962, 23:2, pp. 48-67. *See also* Jansek, Eigor. "Faster Than Flesh: Rotting Speeds of Various Moral Attitudes." *Scientific Reprints Series IV*. Eigor Press: New York. 1976.
Evidence does point, too, to women artists *idealizing* young male corpses, and conceiving. Since these women were themselves *pre-mortem*, however, tomb-watching church societies could keep no tabs on these births. Their cases remain largely conjectural.

10   Huntly, John. *Disease and Virginity*. The Riverside Press: Cambridge. 1884. Huntly does mention the obscure sect that promoted marriages between living men and dead child-brides: for the virginity guaranteed thereby pointed toward a truly heavenly relationship, in which the husband acquired in perpetuity the purity of virginity in his wife.

11   Hibberling, Lisa. "Collars of Cloth — or Brass: Pro-Progress Ecclesiastics and the Kipling Question." *Kipling Studies*. May 1964, 25:4, pp. 40-8.

12   Pines-Sawyer, Etta. *Throttled by a Thurible Chain: How the Anti-Kiplings Incensed William Morris*. Norwalk Academy Press: Norwalk, Wisconsin. 1992.

13   Some artists did anticipate this. Perhaps the most famous example is painter of miniatures Andrew Allweather Derby-Pines, of Manchester, who began signing his works "Andy Lee." Although art historians have identified him as clearly *not* a kipling, he nevertheless won a place for himself in historical accounts for his efforts to dupe posterity.

14   Kipling, op. cit., p. 3.

15 Ibid., pp. 3, 64. Also p. 57, where she says, "It's my work, — mine, — mine, — mine! I've been alone all my life in myself, and I'm not going to belong to anybody except myself."

16 Ibid., p. 5. Saying "nothing is sacred" is akin to saying "everything is equally sacred," a pantheistic attitude.

17 Ibid., p. 9.

18 Ibid., op. cit., pp. 11-2.

19 Ibid., pp. 46, 5. Oddly enough, in this Albatross edition, in the "brass collar" passage that ends Chapter One, pp. 11-2, Amomma's name is misspelled Ammoma — like "ammo." Industrial-society technics, in other words, brings about the demise of Maisie's animal soulmate, at least symbolically. Dick as an adult would invoke Jove and Allah, not God; and his ears once he came home from North Africa must have been attuned to hearing Amomma's closeness in sound to *imam* — *priest*, in a Mohammedan mosque. Maisie's guiding light, Amomma, is dead; and Dick's guiding light, Maisie, is as a consequence dead to him.

20 Kipling, op. cit., p. 58.

20-B. Thomson, Jena. *Kipling and Industrialization*. Studies in Industry and Literature No. 33. University Press: Graf, Iowa. 1973.

21 Caladish, Irene. *A Celebration of Melancholies: Exhibition Notes, with a Detailed History of* Melancolias *in European Painting*. Western Arts Council: Pocatello. 1994.

22 Pines-Sawyer, Etta. *Bearded Ladies in Modern Art*. Norwalk Academy Press: Norwalk, Wisconsin. 1996, pp. 32-7.

23 Ibid., p. 35. On p. 16, Pines-Sawyer also asks: "Was she priestlike in any way? In Kipling, Heldar significantly *sees the red-haired girl only on Sundays*."

24 Caladish, Irene. *Anonymous, and Anon. Un-Mustached: A Study, with the Most Thoroughly Detailed History Ever of* Melancolias *in European Painting*. Center for International Arts: Caledonia, Minnesota. 2002.

The Kurtz-Moreau Syndicate

John J. Coyne

He cried in a whisper at some image, at some vision — he cried out twice, a cry that was no more than a breath — "The horror! The horror!"

—Joseph Conrad, Heart of Darkness

The Kurtz-Moreau Syndicate

For other uses, see Kurtz-Moreau (disambiguation)

The **Kurtz-Moreau Syndicate** was an alleged animal trafficking ring operating out of southern Africa during the mid to late 1880s. The syndicate purportedly trapped animals in the African savannah and shipped them, alive, to a remote island in the South Pacific, where they were subject to unspecified scientific processes and subsequently returned to Africa for military purposes. The syndicate is believed to have been run by British mining magnate Cecil Rhodes for the benefit of his private militia.

The primary evidence of the syndicate's existence comes from two manuscripts discovered in a London vault. The manuscripts contain the accounts of two Royal Navy spies describing first-hand encounters with the syndicate's primary operators: an ivory trader named Kurtz, stationed in a remote region of Congo Free State, and a disgraced London scientist living on a remote island in the south Pacific, identified only as Moreau, or "The Doctor."

CONTENTS

The Deptford Vault Manuscripts

Main Article: The Deptford Vault

In early 2012, a team of archeologists from the University College London (UCL) unearthed a vault hidden beneath London's Deptford Strand.[1] Located near the site of the Convoys Wharf, the Royal Navy's first dockyard, researchers at UCL believe that it served as a secret storage locker in or around the 1890s for a Lord Commissioner of the Admiralty, whose identity remains a mystery. [2] Among the contents of the vault were two long, hand-written reports authored by secret agents of the Admiralty, the governing body of the British Royal Navy. The agents who wrote the reports are identified only by code names: Prendick, whose target was Moreau, and Marlow, whose target was Kurtz.

According to Prendick's report, he was dispatched by the Admiralty to the eastern Pacific Ocean near the Equator in early 1887. The ever-suspicious Admiralty had spotted an unusually high volume of freighted schooners in this area of the Pacific flying the flag of Africa's Cape Colony.[3] Believing that they were associated with Cecil Rhodes, who lived in Cape Colony and whose actions were of sufficient significance to warrant the Royal Navy's attention, the Admiralty planned a mission to track the ships to their destination—an island occupied by a British scientist named Moreau.

Less than two years after Prendick returned to London, Marlow, the Admiralty's other agent, was dispatched to the Congo. Although Marlow's report does not mention Prendick, it becomes clear by the end of the report that the intelligence Prendick had brought back from Moreau's island convinced the Admiralty to send a spy directly into Congo's Katanga region. Marlow's mission—to locate and interrogate a rogue militant known as Kurtz—led him far up the Congo River, deep into the interior of the Congo Rainforest, the second largest rainforest in the world.[4]

Marlow departed London in late 1889 on a trading yacht for Boma, a port city in the Congo River basin. He travelled under the guise of a steamboat captain in the employ of a Belgian trading company, under which cover he entered the Katanga region of Congo Free State and tracked down Kurtz.

His encounter with Kurtz, and the ambiguous nature of the information Marlow extracted from him, have sparked controversy within the United Kingdom and elsewhere over the extent to which the British South Africa Company, Cecil Rhodes's vehicle for the colonization of the African continent, planned to challenge King Leopold of Belgium for dominance in the Congo.[5]

The Race for Katanga

The large, mineral-rich Katanga region in Central Africa was the subject of fierce competition between Europe's two most powerful colonial forces: the Congo Free State, controlled by King Leopold of Belgium, and Cecil Rhodes's British South Africa Company.[6]

In 1891, King Leopold sent Captain William Stairs, a Canadian-born British soldier, and 400 other men, primarily Africans, into Katanga province to coerce the local chief of that region, Mwenda Msiri, into signing a treaty giving Leopold rights to mine the region.[7]

Rhodes, meanwhile, attempted to mount an expedition of his own, but held back for reasons that contemporaries attribute to an intervention by the British government.[8] The precise reasons for such an intervention—and why Rhodes abided by it—have been the subject of long-standing debate among historians.[9] The Kurtz-Moreau documents discovered in the Deptford Vault, however, indicate that Rhodes may have been planning a strong challenge to Leopold and Msiri in Katanga—involving a secretive militia of surgically enhanced beasts—only to see his plans foiled by the Admiralty.

Prendick's Report

In his report, Prendick claims to have studied Moreau for months, collecting newspaper clippings and casually befriending former colleagues of his. Moreau had scandalized London nearly ten years earlier when an animal he had been vivisecting escaped onto the streets of London.[10] The Admiralty traced Moreau from London, from which he fled shortly after his public disgrace, to a small island off the western coast of South America, near an unusually busy sea lane.

Prendick opens his report with a description of the ruse he undertook to smuggle himself onto Moreau's island and gain the confidences of the secretive scientist. In the spring of 1887, Prendick departed London aboard a Royal Navy gunboat bound for the South Pacific. The gunboat dropped anchors a day's journey out from Moreau's island, at which point Prendick, disguised as the victim of a shipwreck, boarded a battered pram and set a course that would intersect the nearby sea lane. His plan was to be "rescued" by one of Moreau's ships and taken to the island as an unwitting guest. The report describes the elaborate measures he took to convincingly assume the appearance of a shipwreck survivor:

> I pushed off from the gunboat twenty nautical miles out from the lane where my Moreau trafficked. With the wind blowing six knots into my sail, I had plenty of time to concoct a convincing appearance. My clothing had already frayed and was stained from ten straight days of continuous use aboard the HMS ____, supplemented by careful tears and burns. My cover story—that I was the sole survivor of the wreck of the *Lady Vain*—had already been fed to the London papers. Now, in the sun, I smeared castor oil over my exposed limbs so as to concentrate the sunlight onto my already sea-reddened skin. Finally, so as to satisfy any dubious minds as to the extent of the ordeal I would claim to have undergone, I took a rod of pig iron

and administered several hard wallops to my extremities. Twelve hours later, when the schooner, the *Ipecacuanha*, found me and took me aboard, I was ripe as a Kentish plum and nearly out of my mind.

Once "rescued" by the *Ipecacuanha*, Prendick found himself sharing passenger quarters with an Englishman named Montgomery and another man that Prendick described as a "deformed mutt of a man, with a face full of black hair." Montgomery introduced this oddly disfigured man to Prendick as his assistant. The captain, a drunkard named Davis, took unhappily to Prendick's presence aboard his ship and insisted that he remain on deck and away from his cargo. Among the cargo that Prendick was able to ascertain from deck was a caged <u>puma</u>.

Prendick introduced himself to Montgomery as a London-based biologist. He claimed to be on his way to the <u>Isla del Coco</u> to embark on a multi-year study of the island's native fauna when a typhoon off the coast of Ecuador destroyed his ship.

Davis dropped anchor about two nautical miles off the shore of a small island. A large boat was dispatched from the island to carry Montgomery, his assistant, and the puma to shore. Montgomery initially refused to allow Prendick to accompany them to the island, and ordered Captain Davis to drop him at the first port he returned to. But as their boat pulled away from the *Ipecacuanha*, Prendick flung himself over the stern and began to swim towards Montgomery's boat. When Montgomery brought the boat back to rescue him, Prendick claimed that Captain Davis threw him overboard before raising anchor.

In his report, Prendick notes that the men who accompanied Montgomery to shore were disfigured in the same way as Montgomery's assistant. As they rowed back to shore, Prendick meditates on their ghastly appearance:

> They had lank black hair, almost like horsehair, and seemed as they sat to exceed in stature any race of men I have seen. None were taller than myself; but their bodies were

abnormally long, and the thigh-part of the leg short and curiously twisted. They were an amazingly ugly gang...

Shortly after reaching shore, Montgomery reluctantly introduced him to Moreau. Knowing of Moreau's interest in <u>evolutionary biology</u>, Prendick, in the guise of a travelling biologist, told Moreau that he was a student of <u>Thomas Henry Huxley</u>, an English biologist and acolyte of Darwin who was also Moreau's mentor. As Prendick had predicted, Moreau's curiosity about his former mentor, and his desire to hear of recent advances in the field of evolutionary biology—which Prendick had studied intensively as preparation for his mission—overcame Moreau's suspicions, and Moreau began to take him into his confidence.

Moreau allowed Prendick to stay in a small room with two doors: one facing out to the island, the other facing the interior of a complex with tall wooden walls, which was locked from the outside. The interior, Montgomery tells him, was off limits to all but himself and Moreau. The following day, Prendick awoke to the sound of an animal crying out in pain:

> After having researched the mechanics of Moreau's business so thoroughly, I had believed myself inured to the horrors of <u>vivisection</u>. Alas, the poor creature's shrieks sent a chill through my bones. What manner of monster can simply *torture* one of God's creations so? I took advantage of both Moreau's and Montgomery's absence and sought refuge in the jungle.

Prendick wandered alone for the better part of the day, and observed several more of the deformed animal-like people he had already encountered. One such person Prendick described as an "ape man" who, despite his beast-like appearance, spoke comprehensible English and proved to be especially gregarious.

This ape man took Prendick to a colony within the jungle filled with others just like him. There, this beast, who called himself the "Sayer of the Law," subjected Prendick to a lengthy litany of laws, which included prohibitions against walking around on "all fours," chasing men, and being unclean.

As Prendick listened to this litany of the beast men's laws, he arrived at a realization about Moreau:

> This man has made himself a god on this island: a minor deity with a deformed, feral flock. I realized then that if I was to get any operational intelligence out of him, wits alone would not suffice; it would require nothing short of brute force.

Prendick fled the ape men in the middle of his recitation and returned to Moreau's compound. The shrieking of the animal had by that time subsided, though Prendick still wrote that "stifled moans and guttural hacks that, if anything, were more chilling than the poor beast's screams, continued to emanate from within the compound." He found a revolver in a trunk in Montgomery's room, shot through the door to the inner courtyard, and interrupted Moreau and Montgomery in the process of vivisecting a puma—the same one that was on board the *Ipecacuanha*. Immediately upon interrupting Moreau and Montgomery at their work, Prendick writes:

> Before they could speak one word, I aimed the revolver at Montgomery's right knee and fired. My savior-at-sea collapsed onto the ground with a shriek that rivaled that of the poor puma, which was still laid up on Moreau's table, layers of flesh peeled away like bed sheets and the animal's pink inner muscle still throbbing in agony.
>
> "Prendick," Moreau shouted, "have you lost your fucking mind?"
>
> In response, I took aim at Moreau's left knee and gave him the same as Montgomery. As the two were squealing in pain on the ground, I approached the poor puma and put her out of her extended misery. I removed her from the table and, in her place, strapped down Moreau.

He goes on to describe, in a level of detail that borders on fetish, conducting a vivisection of Moreau himself:

> Upon securing the leather fasteners to his arms and legs, I cut his clothes away. Moreau merely choked and warbled, his mind still on his shattered knee. But when I took hold of his scalpel and sank it into the skin beneath the hollow of his throat he quieted right up.

> He screeched for a good minute, at the end of which, panting for breath, he mouthed the words "What...do you...want?" between short, rapid breaths.

> "Tell me," I said, holding his gaze, "about your client in Africa."

> "Ahh... Africa?" Moreau sputtered. Making a swift incision through the skin of the sternum, I commenced my first experiment in vivisection. I had barely reached his navel when my poor old host rediscovered how to talk, and within a minute he was chatting away like a man trying to clear his conscience. He proceeded to describe to me the purpose of the cape Colony schooners calling at his island.

> "They bring animals, from Africa." His breathing had become labored, and a mistaken slip of my scalpel had rendered his voice box rough and gurgley. "I am to make him an army of beasts."

> "Him *who*?" I asked, drawing the scalpel further down his belly. "Tell me whom you work for!"

> "His name..." Moreau shrieked as I reached his pubic bone, "is Kurtz. Oh God—Kurtz! In the Congo!"

> "Very good," I said, slowing the scalpel's progress down his belly. "And exactly what kinds of services do you render this Mr. Kurtz?"

> "Beast men," Moreau wheezed. "He sends me beasts— fabulous beasts from darkest Africa—and I give them the

minds of men. Simple men, but fierce. The simple ones make the fiercest soldiers."

"Soldiers?" I asked. I wanted to laugh but couldn't find it in me. By now I was getting good and soaked in the good Doctor's blood, and I knew I had his attention for only a few more moments, at best. "How is that even possible?"

"You forget all that a skilled vivisector can do with living things," said Moreau. "Just look around this island. You've met some of them already, yes?"

"These creatures," I said, looking over my shoulder as if they were staring at the back of my head, "are not men but beasts that you have transformed?"

"Yes, but these are but the trivial cases, the rejects, the ones Kurtz doesn't want. He wants only the best."

"And what, exactly," I asked, "does Kurtz need with an army of beast men?"

"Tiger cock-spurs..." Moreau muttered, already on the far side of delirium from his lost blood.

"Moreau," I shouted, "tell me, who is Kurtz!"

"Rhinoceros rats..."

I took the scalpel and placed it below his eye socket. Getting close to his ear, I whispered, "Kurtz! Tell me about Kurtz!" as the blade slowly pierced the soft flesh.

But it was no good, Moreau was lost. He began to hum "God Save the Queen," every few words punctuated by frightful sputtering as blood fought with the words to exit his mouth.

Prendick's report ends with his disposal of Moreau's and Montgomery's bodies. On his last night there, Prendick found a bottle of <u>rum</u> in Moreau's quarters and, after drinking a third of it, attempted to befriend the mutants who had taken to following him around at a distance. Under the effects of alcohol, the mutants became violent and began to destroy Moreau's encampment. Fearing for his safety, Prendick boarded the boat that had carried him to shore and departed the island just as a fire enveloped Moreau's compound. He fired three flares and was met half a day later by the Royal Navy gunboat, which had been circling the island at a safe distance.

Marlow's Report

Marlow's report begins with his arrival in the Congo port town of Boma. There, he contracted as a steamboat captain with a Dutch trading firm and was sent to a trading station further up the Congo River to await his assignment.

From the moment he lands at Boma, Marlow devotes page after page to his encounters with enslaved native Africans. The early part of his report abounds with descriptions of their emaciated "dark shapes" wearing nothing but "black rags around their loins," with bodies so malnourished that their "every rib rose from their torsos like fingers laced in prayer." At times Marlow's fascination with the enslaved Africans inspires passages of dense, quasi-poetic philosophizing:

> We are accustomed to look upon the shackled form of a conquered monster, but there—there you could look at a thing monstrous and free. It was unearthly, and the men were— No, they were not inhuman. They howled, and leaped, and spun, and made horrid faces; but what thrilled you was just the thought of their humanity—like yours—the thought of your remote kinship with this wild and passionate uproar. Ugly."

The attention Marlow pays to the enslaved Africans initially led researchers charged with examining the Deptford Strand manuscripts to conclude that he had been tasked with reporting on the condition of the African people under the control of the Belgians.[11] It becomes apparent only later on in his report that his mission is far more specific, and that this opening passage seems to reflect only Marlow's grotesque fascination with the people of the Congo. Indeed, Marlow's thinly veiled revulsion to any individual with black skin—enslaved or otherwise—is apparent throughout his report.

Marlow asked after Kurtz among the Dutch traders at his trading post. While every one of them had heard of Kurtz—indeed, Marlow quickly discovered that the prodigious quantities of ivory coming from his station had earned Kurtz a place in local legend—no one was able to give him precise information regarding Kurtz's whereabouts.

Marlow treated all of the legends and rumors of Kurtz with a curious skepticism, not so much expressing uncertainty about the veracity of the claims but constantly hinting at an ulterior motive behind their existence. Describing a conversation with the trading company's accountant, who boasts that Kurtz "sends in as much ivory as all the others put together," Marlow cynically notes "Genius indeed! His cover story has made him famous."

Stranger still, when one day Marlow awoke to find his steamboat has sunk, his account of the matter is suffused with the certainty that his mission has been deliberately sabotaged as a result of his inquisitiveness over Kurtz. "I have perhaps exposed my hand," he writes. "From here on out, my tongue shall remain clenched firmly between my teeth, and I shall be merely an observer."

It took several months to repair his ship. By the time Marlow had returned it to working condition, the company had handed down his orders. Through what Marlow described as a "remarkable piece of good fortune," he was to make his way up river to a station that the Dutch chief of the trading station calls "Kasteel Kurtz." There, he was to locate the elusive Kurtz and return with him to the station, where the station chief intended to "have some words with him" regarding what he called "erratic and dangerous behavior."

Marlow's journey up the Congo was fraught with disease, racial tensions, and near disasters. After a week on the water, and as they were nearing the point on the map marking Kurtz's location, a barrage of arrows assaulted Marlow's ship from the jungle. A member of Marlow's crew was killed in the assault — a black man whom Marlow, in his report, describes with uncharacteristic fondness. Marlow surmised that Kurtz had received word about Marlow's mission to apprehend him and ordered his boat attacked. "I decided to take matters into my own hands," he writes.

> I jumped from the taffrail, where I stood when the attack began, and ordered the boat to proceed onward at full-speed. Accompanied by the smack of arrows against the hull, I dove to my quarters and grabbed my Martini-Henry and a sack of bullets. I strapped my machete to my leg and, from my cabin window, began picking off the attackers one by one. Once we had passed them by a safe distance, I ordered the boat ashore at a clearing and, not waiting for the crew, disembarked. I was intent on finding Kurtz, and would take down anyone who stood in my way.

Marlow followed the clearing up to an assemblage of palm thatch cabins. He found no white men there, only Africans. He threatened several of them with physical harm unless they told him where he could find Kurtz. He claims to have "gone through three of them before they finally accompanied me — like visiting royalty — to the great man's abode." As he entered Kurtz's cabin, Marlow recounts its most striking feature: "Nearly two dozen severed heads stood upon pikes encircling the hut. The black skin of the faces was barely visible through the clouds of flies. Curiously, all but one was facing in toward the house."

Inside, Marlow finally set eyes upon Kurtz. In stark contrast to the dashing man of legend Marlow has heard about from dozens of people, he found instead a man delirious, weak with disease, and near death:

> I was clearly looking at a man straddling the boundary between this world and the next. My entrance seemed to have roused him from a slumber, but he merely looked at

me with wide, peaceful eyes and smiled. After a minute wherein the two of us silently beheld one another, he spoke. "You are, I presume, the man sent by the company to take me to heel."

"Yes and no," I said, my hand feeling for the handle of my machete. "At least, I'm not looking to take you away."

Kurtz turned his head and beheld me with some curiosity. "You _were_ that chap in the steamer, were you not?"

"Indeed," I said.

"Then, if you're not from the company, what do you want from me?"

I stepped closer to his cot until I was nearly standing above his head. "I want to know about the animals," I said.

"The elephants, dear boy?" He laughed. "Why, we tusk 'em! What's there to know?"

"No," I told him. I brought my mouth up close to his ear and whispered, "The beast men, you fool. From the Doctor's Island." Kurtz's already pale face turned nearly transparent when I uttered those words, and his eyes, liquid and frenetic with fever, nearly dribbled from their sockets.

We beheld each other in silence for another minute before he closed his eyes and let out a deep breath. "How much do you know?" he asked.

"We know about the ships of live beasts leaving Boma. We know about the Doctor, and the things he does to them. We know about the island."

When I mentioned the island his eyes shot open and shone on me like great beacons of light. "The island!" he cried. "Have you actually been there?"

"No," I replied. "But men of my organization have, and they have sent me here to extract certain information from you, one way or another." I pulled my machete from its strap and held it by my side, but Kurtz paid neither it nor me any mind. His head angled up at the cabin ceiling, and his eyes seemed to peer through it up into the African sky. His skin had blanched a paler shade of white.

"Tell me," Kurtz said, "the Island, is it still there?"

"The island? Yes. But everything else on it—and everyone else on it, man and beast and otherwise—have been consigned to flame.

Kurtz's head sank into his chest. "All is lost, then, in Katanga. Old Leo appears to have won the day."

After this utterance, no threat I made could return his attention to me. I battered him and cut him, but he took no notice. Finally I dropped my weapon, took him by his arms and shook him. Only then did Kurtz's eyes fall on me again, and they were cloudy pink and wild.

He cried in a whisper at some image, at some vision—he cried out twice, a cry that was no more than a breath— "The horror! The horror!"

A bout of violent coughs set a slow trickle of blood flowing from the corner of his lips. He lurched up out of his cot and seized the neckline of my shirt. I pushed him back down and, blowing out the candle next to his bed, left the cabin for the mess-room. A continuous shower of small flies streamed upon the lamp, upon the cloth, upon our hands and faces. Suddenly the manager's boy put his insolent black head in the doorway, and said in a tone of scathing contempt— "Mistah Kurtz—he dead."

Marlow's report contains no further mention of his interaction with Kurtz. Instead, he concludes with a description of his return journey down the Congo, where, he writes, "I returned uneventfully to London, whose black clouds and tranquil waters welcomed me back to the darkness."

Controversy

Kurtz's mention of Katanga in Marlow's report has raised a number of questions concerning the period of European occupation and colonization of Africa known as The Scramble for Africa.

Scholars studying the Deptford manuscripts have claimed that the true reason for Rhodes's failure to take Katanga in 1892 was a sudden lack of military force. Kurtz, they claim, was building an army of surgically-enhanced animals for use in Katanga and in other colonization efforts. Prendick's assassination of Moreau and the subsequent destruction of the island's facilities reversed Rhodes's entire military strategy in a single blow.[citation needed] Leopold's success in Katanga and elsewhere, and the resulting horrors he visited upon the inhabitants of the territories under his control, came at the expense of the British South Africa Company.

Identities of the Agents

Although there is little evidence about the identities of Marlow and Prendick, speculation has focused on a Pole, Józef Teodor Korzeniowski, a naturalized British sea captain, and Herbert Wells, a London zoologist and school teacher.[12] Both men match rough profiles of Prendick and Marlow, and both are unaccounted for during the time periods covered in their reports. Wells took an extended leave of absence from his teaching job in 1887, returning the following year with lingering health problems.[13] Korzeniowski, a sea boat captain by profession, had signed on as a steamboat captain in the Congo in 1889, placing him at the right place and right time.[14]

The Kurtz-Moreau Syndicate in Popular Media

The _Hollywood Reporter_ blog recently claimed that J. J. Abrams has started filming a movie based on the Kurtz-Moreau Syndicate.[15] According to the web site, James Franco is playing Prendick, and Jeff Bridges has been cast as Marlow. Colin Firth will be playing Kurtz. Abrams is rumored to have reworked the script to replace Moreau with a female character named Mora, played by Audrey Tautou.

The Kurtz-Moreau Syndicate was parodied in the 29th season of The Simpsons, where Homer is Prendick and Mr. Burns is Kurtz.[16]

Notes/References

1   Roswell, Sharon. "Excavations of the Deptford Strand: A New Vantage on Imperial Britain." _The Journal of the British Archaeological Association_ 89, 206 (2015).

2   Wolferstan, Wallace. "Parsing the Mysteries of the Deptford Vault." _UCL Institute of Archaeology._ 125, 38 (2017).

3   Cornwell, Magnus (2018). _Secrets within Secrets: A History of Great Britain's Military Spy Complex._ Gramsci Press, Turin, p. 606.

4   "The Congo rainforest of central Africa." Greenpeace: http://www.greenpeace.org.uk/forests/congo.

5   Haile, Rahawa. "Everything that's Rhodes is New Again." _The Cascadia Subduction Zone_ 5, 19: (2015).

6   Galbraith, John S. (1974). _Crown and Charter: The Early Years of the British South Africa Company._ University of California Press, Berkley. p. 251.

7   Moloney, Joseph Autustus (1893). _With Captain Stairs to Katanga, 1891-92._ British Library, Historical Print Editions, London p. 183.

8   Katzenellenbogen, S. E. (1973). *Railways and the copper mines of Katanga*. Clarendon Press, Oxford. p. 8.

9   Kahanovich, David. "Cecil Rhodes and the Aborted Katanga Expedition: A Reassessment." *Journal of British Studies* 76, 1 (2016).

10 unattributed. "Madman's Beasts Terrorize Kensington." *The Illustrated Police News*. 5 May 1882: 1+.

11 Roswell (2015).

12 Yourcenar, Peggy. "Sleuthing Out the Men in the Vault." *Seattle Review of Books* 21 September 2016, 57-64.

13 Ibid.

14 Ibid.

15 Norris, Nigella. "The Dude Goes to Katanga." *Thehollywoodreporter.com*, 19 March 2018.

16 McHugh, Beryl. "Homer and Marge Wrap up Decade Three: A Peek at the Simpsons Season 29." *Thehollywoodreporter.com*, 20 December 2018.

Dejah Thoris

Mark Rich

Dejah Thoris

Dejah Thoris is a figure of paradox, claiming the title of a book in which she only sporadically appears: *A Princess of Mars*, by Edgar Rice Burroughs. Her power over readers in those sporadic appearances, however, launched Burroughs as a popular novelist. That she is other than purely fictional suggests itself in her reappearances in other seminal works of the imagination.

Life

Dejah Thoris, a Martian Princess of Helium, is an ambassador sent with a flotilla of egg-shaped sky-ships to obtain peace in another part of Mars. She is captured and humiliated—and rescued and captured again—and rescued and at last joined with military hero John Carter, an Earthman. The two produce an offspring: a Martian egg.

Name

Analyses of her name take several approaches. Most commentators believe it reveals her nature—as in the interpretation that Dejah is a version of *déjà*, meaning *already* or *previously*.[i] Some critics, who see her as an H. Rider Haggard-type reincarnation figure, believe her name refers to her recurring presence through time.[ii] Others argue that Dejah Thoris is *already* or *previously* due to her status as a near-immortal among the Martians.[iii] <u>Hans Dunlap Pines</u>'s identification of Martian writings that suggest "Thoris" means "and ever after" or "and then later," while fitting, is set aside by most critics because of the dubious nature of the "runes" Pines supposedly found within a meteorite of metamorphosed sedimentary origin.[1] The fact that Dejah Thoris was, and perhaps is, an inhabitant of a mythic Mars, not the hypo-mythical planetary Mars that is ours to see in night skies, adds further to arguments against the relevance of Pines's discovery, whether or not authentic. Most interpreters, however, agree that the *déjà* reading neatly conjoins the reading that Dejah is a variant on words common to many languages referring to the heavens, such as *deus*, *deva*, *dia*, and even *Diana*, the Roman goddess who, in common with Dejah, embodies and represents the salvation of a race through childbirth and royal succession. Indeed, Dejah Thoris makes her first appearance in a chapter entitled "A Fair Captive of the Sky."

Characteristics

That Dejah Thoris is related to Diana and, in fact, may herself be a Martian goddess explains her survival in battles during which all others on her side are exterminated, and also her ability to beget a child with a member of a different planet's species — or, in mythological terms, with a mortal. Although mortal-immortal crossbreeding has vanished from sub-mythological Earth — the planet most readers presumably inhabit, it being the one given us for at least two millennia — it once proved an important element in human history, with Europe herself born of such a union.

Several characteristics emerge from the main source for details about her, Burroughs's *A Princess of Mars*. Tellingly, the title indicates its subject is the Princess herself, although its main character and *apparent* subject is John Carter, an adventurer from the American South. Carter is a personification of a Western deity of Early Modern times: for he is Duty — a mythic figure under-recognized in our Postmodern times and, in fact, suspected dead, given the deity's public symbolic death in the Kennedy assassinations. On Earth, Carter is simply another postbellum Southern gentleman—i.e., a complicated figure compounded of pride, guilt, and greed, who may be on the run from Northerners who recalled his role in the US Civil War. Once transported mystically to Mars,[2] however, Carter becomes a purified version of himself, physically possessed of powers beyond the experience of Martians, and, as noted, the embodiment of Duty. While a common soldier, he undergoes a series of trials[3] that prove him worthy of the love of the Princess.

Burroughs describes her physically as Everywoman: "a slender, girlish figure, similar in every detail to the earthly women of my past life"—with "of my past life" a clever reference to *previously*. Burroughs then contrasts this Everywoman aspect with the influences of the Ideal: "Her face was oval and beautiful in the extreme, her every feature was finely chiseled and exquisite, her eyes large and lustrous, and her head surmounted by a mass of coal black, waving hair... Her skin was of a light reddish copper color, against which the crimson glow of her cheeks and the ruby of her beautifully molded lips shone with strangely enhancing effect." That she went about essentially naked, too, constituted a Classical-style evocation of divine vision: "nor could any apparel have enhanced the beauty of her perfect and symmetrical figure."[4]

Dejah Thoris herself remains away from the action of this "novel," by and large. While Burroughs might be and has been described as a writer unable to write realistically of women, *A Princess of Mars* is an early work and as such may contain privileged content. [5] In its pages Burroughs discovered the best means for depicting Woman, as opposed to women—which is by omission. In keeping with Classic tradition, Burroughs wrote with averted eyes, much as a newspaper reporter would in whipping up a feature on Diana's sacred rites, upon which it is death to gaze. Dejah Thoris, however, could appear to readers in her mortal guise, as when she is threatened and held roughly captive by enemy warriors, or when she is placed as alluring prisoner before a slavering giant enemy

Thark who evinces sexual desires. She is, in such scenes, absolutely beautiful and absolutely subjugated *except in spirit*. Her
physicality and mortal qualities are exaggerated of necessity by
Burroughs, who has no other means of revealing the fact that
he is writing about divinity—no other means, that is, than his
technique of *sequential absences*, which allowed him to extend
the Dejah Thoris *spirit* through the many pages of the novel from
which physically she goes completely absent. That Burroughs did
succeed, by this means, in offering an authentic vision of Dejah
Thoris to the world becomes apparent from examining his large
catalog of novels, all of which depict actions swirling violently
around Ideals without actually offering to readers the deadly-to-
behold Ideals themselves.

As a purely secular writer Edgar Rice Burroughs, or "ERB," wrote
the most mystical, perhaps even most religious, novels of the
early twentieth century. Some regard it as not coincidental that
he was writing at the time evangelical novels of the coming Rapture were first becoming popular and winning readers to Funda-
mentalist beliefs,[6] and argue that Burroughs's approach, against
that of the evangelical novelists, had greater religious influence
in the United States, despite the fact that the Erbivorian Church,
founded in Albuquerque in 1946, was relatively short-lived. The
Dejah Thoris Chapter of the Erbivorians, a longer-lived manifesta-
tion of Burroughs-influenced belief structures, did issue a long
series of reprints of Burroughs novels and many tracts relating
to the idealistic content and underlying religious nature of Burroughs's works.[7]

Religion

Although many documents disappeared after the burning of the
Erbivorian Church of Albuquerque building, most accounts of
church activities agree on several points. Its origins were twofold,
one being the appearance at the entrance to an Arizona cave of an
apparition seen by several, including a policeman. The apparition

identified herself as Dejah Thoris, who had come to Earth to deliver an egg that held promise for the future. In *A Princess of Mars*, once married to John Carter, she had given birth in normal Martian fashion, by laying a large "snow-white egg." Although the Arizona apparition's egg was never found, Clara Boyd, a cave-event spectator of American Indian descent who subsequently became a church founder, discovered, deep within that cave, egg fragments that scientists failed to pin to any known species.

The second point of origin was publication of the first tract by Hans Dunlap Pines. Pines was a large, impressive man who often dressed formally in black, and whose voice came in for frequent comparison to the wheezings of a pipe-organ's bellows. His tract *On the Origin of Non-Species* suggested that trans-species, interplanetary love held the secrets to world peace and a brighter future.[8] After founding the church, with Boyd and others, Pines witnessed the desert impact of a meteorite that, when recovered, split along a structural planar cleavage, revealing that it was a mineralized text bearing thousands of runes. His initial, partial translation of the runes in 1953 offered evidence that Burroughs had mystically revealed certain aspects of truth concerning Dejah Thoris, albeit within the context of an adventure novel. It also suggested that Dejah Thoris, an immortal spirit, would enter the soul of others after Burroughs, to revitalize them with visionary insight.

Once established, the church embraced the Diana aspect of Dejah Thoris, offering meditation rooms in which supplicants hoping for fertility or success in childbirth could meditate upon the egg images found in *A Princess of Mars* and *Empress: The Meteorite Manuscript*. A lifelike statue of John Carter may have played a part in some meditations. Controversy surrounding these meditation rooms reached their height around the time the church burned.

Legacy

Some argue that the greatest literary relics connected to Dejah Thoris disappeared in the fire: one, the runic stone slabs and

Pines's notes toward a full translation; and the other, papers contained in a shoebox sent in 1948 to Pines by an admirer living in upstate New York.[8-B] This admirer had discovered in the attic what he said was a forgotten family treasure: the missing middle section of F. Scott Fitzgerald's *The Great Gatsby*. According to Pines, these chapters presented readers with a Long Island Princess character whose presence, intended to bring peaceful resolution to a conflict, instead causes the pivotal car accident. While this claim stretches belief, a sample of the manuscript paper Pines sent to a lab matched exactly a sample of Fitzgerald's original manuscript. Pines's argument, moreover, has gained weight with literary historians: for Dejah Thoris makes her "appearances" in novels by sequential *absences*; and Fitzgerald's literary sense told him to leave out this episode from his novel—resulting in the most famous narrative gap among Modern novels.

Perhaps stranger than this, would-be writers felt a deep attraction to the Erbivorian belief system, and nursed hopes that the church's tutelary spirit would introduce sequential gaps into their writings. In our more cynical times the notion evokes sheer disbelief. In the late 1950s and early '60s, however, numerous writers, especially pulp-fiction writers, made pilgrimages to Albuquerque to join the Dejah Thoris Chapter, which held regular, open-to-public meditation sessions around a large marble egg. Although many of these writers later became famous in the science fiction and fantasy genre, relatively few claimed to have found their careers helped by Erbivorian meditations.

The Dejah Thoris Chapter dissolved in the early 1960s, shortly after publication of a work in which Dejah Thoris clearly appears, which made its author a nearly overnight sensation among aficionados. That the author had no connection to any Erbivorian Chapter disheartened many adherents. Subsequent dwindling attendance made it impossible for the organization to continue. Although pockets of belief would hold on for decades, the Erbivorian faith for all practical purposes ended in 1963, the year *The Magazine of Fantasy and Science Fiction* published "A Rose for

Ecclesiastes," by <u>Roger Zelazny</u>. This magazine had been under a constant watch by Erbivorians, due to its initials, *F&SF*, being the same as F. Scott Fitzgerald's. Although in this novelette Dejah Thoris bears the name Braxa, she is symbolically the "Rose" of the title of a story in which she barely appears. She is "redheaded," and in her first appearance is "wearing, sari-like, a diaphanous piece of the Martian sky." Her hidden divinity appears when Earth-poet Gallinger compares her to "a feathered crucifix hovering in the air."[9] Braxa becomes pregnant by Gallinger, the larger-than-life Earthman who occupies the story's foreground. Her pregnancy, moreover, is a sign to the dying Martian race that regeneration is upon them. She is Diana, bringing her race salvation through childbirth.

To the Erbivorians, it was most telling that Braxa should be a pure-hearted devotee of Duty. In Burroughs's original novel, Earthman and Marswoman underwent "the ceremony which made Dejah Thoris and John Carter one."[10] While John Carter symbolically became the salvation of Mars, which was the role of his new mate, in this "becoming one" Dejah Thoris took on John Carter's attribute. She became Duty. In "A Rose for Ecclesiastes," the near-immortal ambassador of her race, Braxa, dissembles love and joins in sex with the Earthman out of tradition-bound Duty. Braxa's caretaker nurse-figure—also an analog of a Burroughs character—speaks with the Earthman, who asks:

> "Then she does not love me? Never did?"
>
> "I am sorry, Gallinger. It was the one part of her duty she never managed."
>
> "Duty," I said flatly. ... Dutydutyduty! Tra-la![11]

Even more distressing to Erbivorians, the Dejah Thoris spirit seemed intent on remaining an inspiration for this non-Erbivorian writer: for the next year, Zelazny published his novella "The Grave-yard Heart." While it ends with pregnancy, the story bears little evidence of the Burroughsian tale—except in its main female character, Leota, who appears in idealized Woman guise, and who seems an airy (for-appearances-only, Beauty and little else). Careful reading, however, reveals that as a character Leota changes steadily throughout the story, being of one nature in one brief appearance, of another nature in her next, and then yet another...so that she obviously goes through the greatest internal struggles of any character within that fictional world. The "Heart" of the title is, moreover, hers. None of Leota's struggles, however, appear before the reader. Leota spirits through the pages by means of brief appearances and *sequential gaps*.

For the devoted few, in 1964 Erbivorian beliefs still reflected universal Truth. Even those few, however, were forced to admit that this Truth had chosen to manifest itself outside Erbivorian circles.

Mars Wars

After the failure of the Chapters, Hans Dunlap Pines moved to Kansas with his two sons, who grew up to nurse writing ambitions of their own. According to the memoir by elder son Ezra, Hans exerted no undue influence on their development as writers, and never imposed Erbivorian beliefs. The sons, in fact, believed the father had put those beliefs behind him.[12] In 1977, however, Hans attended a showing of a science-fantasy movie already winning rave reviews. Although knowledgeable aficionados must have noted the similarities between scenes and names in *A Princess of Mars* and Star Wars, Hans had heard nothing of such comparisons. He was one of sixty-three attendees at the showing in Bird, Kansas, that became a newspaper mini-mystery that summer. At that showing everyone saw the opening title as *Mars Wars*—and saw a movie of violence and high romance, featuring an idealized red-skinned beauty, a Princess Deia who is an ambassador for peace. The Princess goes through capture and reduction to a sexual object before a sluglike enemy creature, Tal Hajus, Jeddak of the Tharks—a scene the likes of which no other viewers would see until the release of a sequel movie years later; and after triumphant victory by her forces the Princess becomes pregnant by the commoner antihero. The film-showing immediately after the one Hans Pines attended began with the title *Star Wars*, unaltered.

When Hans returned home from the theater he telephoned each of his sons, who lived nearby, to say, "I saw Her." Each somehow knew whom he meant. By the time they arrived at his house, their father had settled on a couch, apparently asleep but dead of heart failure. The disappearance of the large white egg displayed prominently in the living room, which prompted a brief criminal investigation, remains a mystery to this day.

Notes/References

i   White, E.G. *Been There, Done That: The Critics and Reincarnation Figures in Modern Novels*. Albumin Editions: New York.

ii Ibid.

iii Ibid.

1   Boyd, Clara. *Martian and Mythic Origins of Space Debris*. M(ars) Press: Albuquerque, NM. Erbivortext No. 9. 1953. Includes a partial runic translation by Hans Dunlap Pines.

2   Boyd, Clara. *Mystical Transport as Sign of Entrance to Myth*. M Press: Albuquerque, NM. Erbivortext No. 28. 1956.

3   Boyd, Clara. *The Jumping of Hoops Even Outside Academia*. M Press: Albuquerque, NM. Erbivortext No. 11. 1954.

4   Burroughs, Edgar Rice. *A Princess of Mars*. The Modern Library: New York. 2003, pp. 49-50.

5   Boyd, Clara, (ed.). *Instinctual Access to Mythic Truth in Early Works of Famous Authors*, 2 Vols. M Press: Albuquerque, NM. Erbivortexts Nos. 12 & 13. 1954-5.

6   Gribben, Crawford. *Writing the Rapture: Prophecy Fiction in Evangelical America*. Oxford University Press: New York. 2009.

7   Pines, Edward, ed. *A Barsoomian Bibliography: The Works of Clara Boyd*. Spent Cartridge Press: Bird, Kansas. 1993. Includes a never-before-published memoir by Hans Dunlap Pines.

8   Pines, Hans Dunlap. *On the Origin of Non-Species*. M Press: Albuquerque, NM. Erbivortext No. 1. 1948. Reprinted with *Empress: The Meteorite Manuscript* as Erbivortext Doubles No. 1. 1961.

8-B. Pines, Edward, ed., 1993, op. cit.

9   Zelazny, Roger. "A Rose for Ecclesiastes." *Four for Tomorrow*. Ace Books: New York. 1967, pp. 183, 185.

10 Burroughs, op. cit., p. 190.

11 Zelazny, op. cit., p. 215. In an unpublished 1964 speech, Hans Pines asserted that Braxas *did* love Gallinger, but that at hearing the words from *Ecclesiastes*, "There is nothing new under the Sun," she-who-was-*previously* then fled, fearing her exposure as Dejah Thoris. In the same speech Pines argued, however, that Leota in "A Graveyard Heart" was *not* Dejah Thoris, because the foreground male commoner figure actually and explicitly *forgets to think about her*, in one part of the story. Despite its cogent argument that Dejah Thoris is *sequentially absent physically but never in spirit*, Pines's speech proved inadequate in its attempt to bolster the disintegrating Erbivorian Chapters.

12 Pines, Ezra. *In Love with Her Shadow: Memories of Dad*. Spent Cartridge Press: Bird, KS. 2004. This account includes the incident in which Hans Dunlap Pines, depressed and perhaps deranged by the failure of the Chapters, accused his son Ezra of having written under Zelazny's name to destroy the church, citing a passage from "A Rose," p. 185: "I was, for a fleeting second, my father in his dark pulpit and darker suit, the hymns and the organ's wheeze transmuted to bright wind." Although "organ's wheeze" might seem a telling reference to his father's voice, Ezra had been a child when Zelazny published the story. This volume also reprints Ezra's

essay, "The Egg-Shaped Soul in Zelazny's _Jack of Shadows_," which contains his controversial claim that he owns a snapshot of Zelazny at home, with what seem to be large fragments of eggshell visible on a shelf behind him.

Mother Hubbard's Cupboard

Anna Tambour

Mother Hubbard's Cupboard

A lot being offered for auction, a collection of useless or possibly valuable things, the term used in the bestselling book *When Time Broke All Bounds*, to refer to the place where objects landed.

CONTENTS

Mother Hubbard in Poetry

Mother Hubbard was, until 1989,[1] commonly thought to be first alluded to by <u>Edmund Spencer</u> in the late 1500s, in his poem "Prosopopoia: or Mother Hubbard's Tale." Although some <u>scholars</u> describe it as a <u>satire</u>,[2] Spencer's fable in verse was never popular, possibly because it is hard to memorize, being 10,953 words, though its 1,442 lines contain 721 simple couplets and preceded <u>free verse</u> by some 300 years. The stanza that we all know in "Old Mother Hubbard" (*Old Mother Hubbard / Went to the cupboard / To get her poor doggie a bone, / When she got there / The cupboard was bare / So the poor little doggie had none*) is only one of many in the poem that has been described as a <u>petition</u> to allow the king to remarry in defiance of the Church's wishes. [3] This poem (that no author has admitted to) has proved to be as much a failure as Spencer's "Prosopopoia" and other Party materials[4] as a means to incite children to politick.[5] Instead, "Old Mother Hubbard," from the coyness of an empty cupboard that should contain a bone to the silliness of a dog wearing spectacles, became a much quoted nursery rhyme published in many editions, not illustrated with pictures of the king, his unwanted wife, and intended replacement, but with amusing pictures of a nice old lady and her attractive canine companion.[6]

Mother Hubbard's cupboard would have sunk into the obscurity of old nursery rhymes but for a burst waterpipe. In 1948, roadworks uncovered what is commonly called "The RCA Manuscript" in a previously unexcavated cellar of the medieval tavern, The Flesshe. This tavern had stood at the junction of what had been, in the Middle Ages, Tyburn Road and Watling Street (Oxford Street and Edgware Road), which means that it must have looked onto "The Tyburn Tree," the busy gallows for common thieves, which had stood at the opposite corner for some hundreds of years. Today, three golden triangles indicate the location of the tree, at the southernmost end of Edgware Road.[7]

The Discovery of the Manuscript

"The RCA Manuscript" (a term that is considered derogatory but has stuck, having quickly edged out the name given it by its primary researcher)[8] is a sheaf of pages that are copiously illustrated and written on in what some scholars think is a personal code. Dating is disputed, but is generally thought to be from around 1330. The handwriting is idiosyncratic, but the pages seem to be a kind of inventory as well as a kind of record of experimentation. Records of ownership have not survived but it has been claimed that The Flesshe was owned at that time by a certain Amelior Hoopart, a Widow.

The dispute about the RCA Manuscript's veracity can never be fully decided. It was accidentally destroyed at the height of the early controversy when a rampant bull's hoof stirred a spark in a compost pile that caught fire beside the shed where Hovian Cuttler had secreted the precious manuscript.[9] But Despenser Hoopart is listed on the tax rolls of the City of London, and he could well have been Amelior's father-in-law. He was known to be an <u>alchemist</u> well ahead of his time,[10] and according to Hovian Cuttler,[11] it was he who instigated the extraordinary occurrences that the RCA Manuscript only touches upon.

The Story Behind the Manuscript

Despenser Hoopart, the alchemist, experimented with many substances in his attempts to turn <u>small beer</u> into <u>gold</u>. It was the unusual corrosiveness of one or more of these that caused, according to Cuttler, "a sundering in the fabric of Time itself."[12] Cuttler hypothesized that the substance was common <u>asparagus</u> that synergized with something stuffed into the boiled cat that Hoopart had placed into the crucible.[13]

Contents of the Manuscript

The pictures in the manuscript are all painted in ink, and are line drawings of a primitive but telling kind. The most famous one, known as the "RCA cartoon," William Beckley[14] claimed to be the subject of a legal dispute between <u>James Thurber</u> and the magazine that would have blown up into a full divorce if Harold Ross hadn't died. The "cartoon" was not, as Thurber supposedly claimed and it certainly appeared to be, a fake Thurber, but was actually a copy of plate 6 from Cuttler's book. It showed an unmistakable resemblance to RCA Victor's newly released Huge Picture Television 9T246 Big 10-inch Picture Tube, Locked in Tone "Eye Witness" Pictures, "Golden throat" tonal brilliance, Simplified Automatic Tuning, Smartly Designed Cabinet, Huge Picture Television, Amazingly low Priced!" which was all the more comical, being so outdated.[15]

There were many disputes about what the drawing could portray, but no other satisfactory explanation was given by experts. Other odd drawings were argued over to no conclusion. These included the following, according to Cuttler and now also, the Society for Transtemporal Importation (STI).[16] These included a pile of <u>antebellum</u> hoops, a clockwork-driven object, the purpose of which was listed in <u>Latin</u> in the first edition of Cuttler's book, and sub-sequently dropped entirely, as was the picture; a "<u>Buck Rogers</u>" screen, handheld; an aerosol can, a small mountain of what Cut-tler theorized were mechanical hands (and they do look as if they are); wands; what looks like a <u>fax machine</u> and they all thought was a "Personal Laundering Device" and sundry items that he and the Society labeled as "Knowledge Creators from the Future."[17]

Pirates of Penzance Connection

An offshoot of the STI formed because of their conviction that the operetta was a parable for the goods smuggled in through the <u>Time Membrane</u> by descendants of Mother Hubbard. "Poor Wan-dering One" sung by Mabel and the chorus of girls,[18] is, by this calculation, referring to the goods, whatever they are, that make their way through Time to land in an often unfriendly and igno-rant Past. No descendants have been proven, and Cuttler was by this time (1958) "unwilling or unable"[19] to participate.

Mother Hubbard's Cupboard Etymology

The term began to be used in British comedy skits within weeks of the launch of *When Time Broke all Bounds*, according to Sydney Brady.[20] Jack Carman and Evangela Crump had a segment on their BBC television show <u>Crumpled Up</u>, in which they pulled out, from a hole in the ground that they called "Mother Hubbard's Cupboard," one hot water bottle after another. The skit is famous because the laughter grew so loud that the banter of the comedians was lost, and Jack lost his temper and shoved one bottle under his arm, is-suing a giant rude fart. He then threw the bottle into the audience as he yelled, "Shut your faces so I can give yous your last laugh." The audience finally went quiet as he stood, clearly angry. He delivered the punchline, and there was silence. Interviewed after-wards, no one in the audience could remember what the punchline referred to since the straight line had been delivered by Evangela so much earlier. Jack never forgave the audience for its timing, and quit television (or was fired).[21]

Recent Events

In October 2012, a seller based in <u>Paris, Texas,</u> offered on e-bay, an item that he said was a find from Mother Hubbard's Cupboard. He stated that it is an Apple device from 2020. From the photo, it is unclear what the device does. It sold for $3,246 to a buyer who has not been revealed.[22]

Notes/References

1   Zehava Zhi-Webb, "Let the Prosopopoia tail fall where it lies: Dehistorating a provenance of unwarranted gain," pp. 245-268. *Proceedings from Bold Disclosures from the Battle of Flodden Field to Pantagruel: Mismythifying 1530-1600 Western Europe, the 10th Conference of the International Society of Literstorians,* Department of Historature, Macawlie University: Adelaide, Australia, 20-24 August 2010. Konstantin Bourke and Opie Kalowitz, eds., Macawlie University Press: Adelaide and Calgary, 2010.

2   <u>http://spenserians.cath.vt.edu/TextRecord.php?action=GET&textsid=115</u>.

3   <u>http://www.rhymes.org.uk/old_mother_hubbard.htm</u>.

4   Jeremy Zilber, *Why Mommy is a Democrat* and *Why Daddy is a Democrat.* <u>http://littledemocrats.net/Democraticbooks.html</u>.

5   C. Douglas Crouch, *Nursery Movements: The Children's-Shield of Political Pampheteering.* IQuo Institute: Ithaca and London, 2003.

6   Read the nursery rhyme here: <u>http://en.wikipedia.org/wiki/Old_Mother_Hubbard</u>.

7   Mortimer Haught, *Swingers Corner.* Thrilling Books: London, 1976.

8   Hovian Cuttler, *When Time Broke All Bounds: The Mother Hubbard's Cupboard Revelations*. Alctimetre Press, Dagenham: Barking and Dagenham, UK, 1950.

9   "Famous author distraught," *Barking Clarion*, p 1, 14 June 1954.

10 Janus Lacinius Therapus, the Calabrian. *A form and method of perfecting base metals, from Giovanni Lacinius Pretiosa margarita novella de thesauro, ac pretiosissimo philosophorum lapide*, Venice, 1546.

11 Hovian Cuttler. *When Time Broke All Bounds: The Mother Hubbard's Cupboard Revelations*, p. 4.

12 Op. cit. p. 20.

13 Op. cit. plate 3A (from the manuscript) p. 44.

14 William Beckley, "Uptown Tattle," *Top Dawgs' Doin's*. Cheap 'n Plenty Publications, 1952.

15 Since the model was already two years old. See the ad in the *New York Herald*. http://www.tvhistory.tv/1950-RCA-Ad-Dec49-NYHerald.JPG.

16 The Society for Transtemporal Importation. *Indisputable Truth; A Handbook for Those of Open Mind*. Chicago, 1951.

17 Gene Hofstadder, *Metamagical Movements*. Sacramento: Inquisitor Publications, 1987.

18 STI Penzancseers, *Manifesto*, 1968.

19 Jackie Forth, *"Another Truth Buried by History." Future Times*, vol. 24, Summer, 2011.

20 Sydney Brady, *Anything for a Larf; Memoirs*. Biddy Head: Chepstow, 1964.

21 H.L. Grescoe and Alice Harrington, "Final Performances." *Annals of Recorded Entertainment*, vol. 67, June, 1999.

22 www.futuresinternational.com/lockedins/-y9035. As of 12 November 2012. This internet site is no longer in service.

Gerayis (or Gedayis)

Alex Dally MacFarlane

Gerayis (or Gedayis)

It was said of Gerayis that as an infant she lapped at the blood in which her grandmother Tomyris placed the head of Cyrus the Great. Though this story was almost certainly a fabrication, crafted by Gerayis herself, among those today who know of Gerayis it is the most commonly told.[1]

Little is known of this queen. Herodotus did not mention her in his *Histories* alongside her grandmother Tomyris and father Spargapises;[2] given her age at the event of Cyrus the Great's final battle, and her more likely location away from the battlefield with the other non-combatants of the Massagetae tribe, this is not surprising. As her marriage took her away from the border of the Achaemenid Empire, she did not feature in any of the Near-Eastern sources, nor in any other written sources — until the 2014 discovery of *Subjugated Peoples*, authored by Herakles. This text is contested in two key areas.[3]

CONTENTS:
1 Subjugated Peoples
2 The Stories of Gerayis
2.1 Early Years
2.2 Queen Gerayis (or Gedayis)
2.3 Death
3 Notes/References

Subjugated Peoples

The papyri comprising the substantial surviving portions of *Subjugated Peoples* were discovered in the desert near Babylon.[4] The author claims to have travelled with Alexander the Great and documented the peoples encountered on the Macedonian army's conquests. To some, this is already the discovery of the century: a contemporary source for Alexander.[5] Others believe the text fits more accurately into the Romance tradition, citing the fantastical nature of some of the peoples encountered, and ascribe to its composition a far later date.[6] Those are the two major arguments, ranging across numerous articles, reviews, and already two books. A smaller number point to the level of detail in the more "realistic" sections and suggest that the text is an interstitial composite of contemporary fact and later fiction.[7]

The second area of contention concerns the gender of Herakles. While the author's name is male, arguments that Herakles was secretly a woman are receiving increased attention.[8]

Subjugated Peoples begins with a clear statement of intent:

> Of the unknown world, there are several known facts: a river or mountain range must be crossed to reach it; the people are often strange, six-legged or winged or ruled by women; there are secrets preserved especially for the people of the known world, placed there by gods or local rulers with little knowledge of what they possessed. Whence these facts came need not be elaborated; they are simply known to all men. Herein I endeavor to lay out the truths of these peoples, whose lives beyond their boundaries with the known world are worthy of their own text. (1.1)

This mission of documenting the "true" lives of the peoples met and subjugated by Alexander's army lent Herakles an open ear; indeed, of the region in which the Massagetae once defeated Cyrus, the author writes: "Stories blow here on the wind like pollen, ready to land on a patch of earth and grow stubbornly despite the often harsh climate in these great reaches" (3.4).

The Stories of Gerayis

Early Years

Of Gerayis the author first reports the popular blood-lapping story: the bloodthirsty infant, grand-daughter of the queen who took great pleasure in punishing the corpse of the man who threatened her people with conquest and death (3.12).

Gerayis is again mentioned in the context of the succession struggle following Tomyris's later death. According to the stories heard by Herakles: "This young princess, said to have rushed out of her mother's womb already on the back of a horse and wielding a fearsome bow, posed such a threat to the princes competing for the rule of the Massagetae that she was sent away to marry a distant king" (3.16). The king's name is never given. "Gerayis honored the grave of her famous grandmother one last time before departing for her husband's lands" (3.17) is all the indication given of her reaction to this effective banishment. How strongly she contested for the Massagetae throne, if at all, is unknown. Working backwards from later stories, at this time she was aged 13 or 14.

Queen Gerayis (or Gedayis)

For the next 20 years, Gerayis's life remains a mystery. Herakles re-introduces her in another story, about a land beyond the reach of even Alexander:

> Now the city of Ta is so distant from the people with whom I sat, that they described it in quite fanciful terms: a city of bones and burnished gold, of vast teeth dangling from the parapets, of rivers running bright with carnelian and turquoise, of people who speak to eagles and feast on the sand that blows in from the desert in great gusts like waves. After all that I have seen, I do not know which of these details to believe.
>
> For many years, a healthy trade existed between the people of the city and the nomadic peoples living on the great plains nearby. The nomadic peoples brought meat and gold and poetry, which they traded in Ta for certain goods that they desired. This process endured peacefully, until a new king began to fear the nomads, who were ruled by a queen with particularly bright eyes: Gedayis,

who could ride a horse faster than any man and shoot an arrow from across great distances. This is surely the Gerayis of the Massagetae, acclaimed for the same skills.

This Gedayis rode into battle with her three daughters, and they were all arrayed with such gold that they gleamed like the sun, which is worshipped by many people in these parts. Each of the daughters was as fearsome as the mother; together, they made whole cities tremble. Convinced that they intended to take his city, this king closed his gates and refused any further trade with the nomads.

After the failure of negotiations, the nomads saw no other choice but to fulfil the king's fears in order to resume their trade. (3.61-64)

What followed was the expected rout. After installing her single son as the wife of the ruler's sister, a set-up that ensured the on-going flow of trade, Gedayis and her army rode back to their home lands (3.65-67).

Of her son, it is then said only that he lacked any appetite for battle, but fared well as a ruler. "The men with whom I sat relished this story," Herakles adds, "applying particular detail to the nature of the women: soaked in blood, hungry for the severed heads of the enemies, even given to copulating with the finest corpses. When I spoke to some of the women, they told a very different story of Gedayis and her children" (3.68). It is this care taken by Herakles to speak with the women — and the very different stories given in these conversations — that suggests a female author.[9]

The women said that all four of Gedayis' children fought with her, enjoying the rush of combat, but behaving in no more disturbing fashion than any other soldier. The son fell in love with the city king's sister, and asked that he might be permitted to live there with her and ensure his people's successful trade; he was no weakling, overshadowed by his fearsome sisters.

The women all agreed that Gedayis and her daughters were formidable, but such is the nature called for by people who must defend their livelihoods. For a female ruler, the need to appear terrifying must be even greater; no doubt this is the origin of her legendary supping of blood. The women agreed that Gedayis and Gerayis were the same, even interchanging their names several times as they spoke. The women then emphasized Gedayis's care for her people and the way she spent her time attending to their concerns, mediating disputes over livestock or brides, sourcing healers for the sick, leading forays against wolves and raiders; and she liked nothing better, they said, than to sit with her children and share the fermented mares' milk that is the preferred drink of her people, singing of sheep and battle and embroidery.

It is said of Gerayis that when she died, instead of falling to the ground, she flung herself into the harsh wind and became a part of it, so that her voice may be heard still, blowing across the plains, singing. I like to fancy that I can hear it—but I am not sure what a woman as admirable as Gerayis could say to me. (3.69-71)

Several further tales of Gerayis followed, but none diverged from the narrative sketched above.

Death

Of her death, Herakles adds a more prosaic story: that an illness took her, late in life, and her children buried her in a grand tumulus not far from a great sea. "Gerayis sang once, of the beauty of horses, her words so mumbled that not even her granddaughter, positioned by her side, heard every word; and then her bowl tumbled from her hand and she died" (3.105).

No other details are attested.

Excavations in 2016 of great mounds 10 km northeast of the Caspian Sea[10] unearthed a series of buried men and women, arrayed gloriously in gold;[11] in one, archaeologists found only a golden comb, a clay bowl, and a horse's skeleton.

Notes/References

1   See, for example, the 10 November 2018 episode of QI.

2   See Herodotus, *Histories*, 1.205-214 for the conflict between Tomyris and Cyrus.

3   For an overview, see Papadatou, A. M. (2017). "Discussing Herakles' *Subjugated Peoples*." In *The Journal of Hellenic Studies* Vol 137: 85-103.

4   "New Alexander History Discovered Near Babylon." *BBC News*. 27 September 2014. Retrieved 13 February 2018.

5   The major arguments are put forward by Sarah Ibi and Hans Bachrach in their book *A Contemporary View of Alexander*. Oxford University Press: Oxford, UK. 2016.

6   See especially the Introduction to the Penguin translation by Helen Kastrisianaki.

7   Towards the end of her JHS 2017 article, A. M. Papadatou argues for this analysis.

8   McCloud, An. (2017) "Herakles or Antigone?" In *The Classical Quarterly*. This argument has resulted in a forthcoming Hollywood adaptation. See http://www.imdb.com/title/tt3156964/. Retrieved 13 May 2018.

9   Ibid.

10 "Treasures Inside Ancient Burial Mounds." *BBC News*. 1 October 2016. Retrieved 15 May 2018.

11 Several examples are on display at the British Museum between September 2018 and February 2019. http://www.britishmuseum.org/whats_on/exhibitions/gerayis.aspx. Retrieved 20 March 2018.

The Galadriel Apocrypha

Kristin King

The Galadriel Apocrypha

The **Galadriel Apocrypha** is a set of stone tablets discovered by the feminist fan cult Sisters of Yavanna in Year 288 of the Fifth Age. According to the <u>Church of the Eleven Queen</u>, these tablets are a hoax and were carved three hundred years after the death of Prophet Tolkien. However, the Sisters claim they merely transcribed Tolkien's unpublished works.

The apocryphal texts include: Galadriel's Question, Galadriel Asks the Powers, Galadriel's Mirror, and Galadriel Leaves Eden.

CONTENTS

Controversy

Both the Priesthood of Ilúvatar and the <u>Church of the Elven Queen</u> maintain that the Galadriel Apocrypha is not only heretical but also a danger to the proper functioning of the Cyborg Sphere. "By valorizing Galadriel's disobedience to the Earthly Powers, the Apocrypha sets Galadriel up in fundamental opposition to the One True Song," wrote High Cyborg Aragorn. The Sisters of Yavanna, however, maintain that all rebellion against Ilúvatar and the Earthly Powers is still part of Ilúvatar's own design.

The characterization of Galadriel is also controversial in these apocryphal texts. They paint a picture of Galadriel as a trans-sexual[1] who befriended the Dark Elves[2] and who was destined to become an organizer and military strategist in a quest to unite all the races of Middle-Earth.[3] This is in direct contradiction to claims made by both the Church of the Elven Queen and the Ilúvatar Priesthood that all elves are strictly heterosexual and respect the Hierarchy of Races, and that any evidence to the contrary stems from serious inconsistencies in Tolkien's unfinished works.[4]

The Ilúvatar AI, as always, has made no comment one way or the other.

Notes

1   Tolkien, Unfinished Tales, p. 241.

2   Ibid. p. 243.

3   Ibid. pp. 246-7, p. 257.

4   Ibid. p. 239.

References

- Author in dispute. *Galadriel Apocrypha*. New York: Yavanna Publications, 288, Fifth Age.
- Tolkien, J.R.R. *Unfinished Tales*. Ed. Christopher Tolkien. New York: Ballantine Books, 1988, Fourth Age.

See Also

- Tolkien, J.R.R. _History of Middle-Earth_. Ed. Christopher Tolkien. 12 vols. New York: Houghton Mifflin, 1983-1996, Fourth Age.

- Bates, Brian. _The Real Middle Earth_. New York: Palgrave Macmillan, 2003, Fourth Age.

Canonical Galadriel

In Year 290 of this Fifth Age, the High Cyborgs of the <u>Church of the Elven Queen</u> came to a decision about which Galadriel texts would become official doctrine. The collection of these texts is known as **Canonical Galadriel.**

"This was a difficult decision," wrote High Cyborg Arwen, "because Prophet Tolkien wrote so many contradictory passages concerning Galadriel. Ultimately we decided that the priority would be on Tolkien's published works. After that, we allowed for a selected set of writings from The History of Middle-Earth, but only where they do not conflict with the published text of the Lord of the Rings or the Silmarillion. Furthermore, in cases where the original penciled text was amended, we chose the amendments."[1]

The canonical texts include:

- Lord of the Rings

- The Silmarillion

- Selected passages from The History of Middle-Earth

Notes

1   Church of the Elven Queen. "High Cyborgs Finalize The Galadriel Canon." _Elven Queen News_, 16 May 290, Fifth Age.

References

- Tolkien, J.R.R. _The Lord of the Rings._ 3 vols. New York: Houghton-Mifflin. 1994, Fourth Age.
- Tolkien, J.R.R. _The Silmarillion._ Ed. Christopher Tolkien. New York: Ballantine Books, 2nd Edition. 2001, Fourth Age.
- Tolkien, J.R.R. _History of Middle-Earth._ Ed. Christopher Tolkien. 12 vols. New York: Houghton Mifflin, 1983-1996, Fourth Age.
- Tolkien, J.R.R. _Canonical Galadriel._ Ed. High Cyborg Arwen. New York: Cyborg Enterprises Unlimited. 290, Fifth Age.

Church of the Elven Queen

The **Church of the Elven Queen** is a highly influential faction of the Cyborg Sphere. It was initially formed as an auxiliary organization to the Ilúvatar Priesthood, also known as the Followers of the All-Father or the Devotees of the One True Song. The Priesthood has since renounced the Church of the Elven Queen as heretical, but the Church maintains that its vision of Galadriel as a faithful servant of Ilúvatar is in full compliance with doctrine.

Galadriel's Question

"Galadriel's Question" is the first of the four Galadriel Apocrypha texts that the Sisters of Yavanna claim to have been written by Prophet Tolkien. This claim is disputed by the Church of the Elven Queen.

Excerpt

Galadriel finished crafting her eight million seven thousand five hundred and sixty-ninth gemstone and wondered, "Am I a slave?" She knew that Melkor was a deceitful and malicious Power, but when he said to the elves that "a slave in a gilded cage is still a slave," his words itched under her skin and made her want to peel away her flesh layer by layer to understand what was inside.

The gemstone glimmered with a cool blue flame and surpassed all her other eight million plus gemstones and jewels and diamonds and marble rocks and so on and so forth—but not by much. Galadriel could say she was still progressing, but it was more true to say that she was standing still, while meanwhile in Middle-Earth, elves and humans were learning and growing.

"Am I a slave?" she asked herself again. Perhaps the question made no sense. According to the Powers, everything in existence was a melody of Ilúvatar's making. She was just a note in a grand and beautiful song. A note has no free will, but is not a slave, only a thing. Is that what she was? The Powers said that one day Ilúvatar would sing the closing note and the Song would be over. He had sung her into existence and could sing her out of it, simply by taking a breath.

Or could He?

The gem she had made was solid and shiny, but when she asked herself questions about Ilúvatar, she could press it between her thumb and index finger, and it would squish like a ripe elderberry, then diminish and fade. If she kept squeezing, would it pop out of existence?

She was afraid to find out.

References

- Author in dispute. "Galadriel's Question." *Galadriel Apocrypha*. New York: Yavanna Publications, 288, Fifth Age.

Galadriel Asks the Powers

"Galadriel Asks the Powers" is the second of the four <u>Galadriel Apocrypha</u> texts that the Sisters of Yavanna claim to have been written by Prophet Tolkien. This claim is disputed by the <u>Church of the Elven Queen</u>.

Excerpt

Manwë and Galadriel knelt over the making-stone, dipping their fingers in the Everlasting fire and swirling it into thousands of luminous colors. Manwë cupped a little of his mixture in his hand and let some drip to his other hand, laughing in delight.

"Galadriel, you try!" With their four hands they made a waterfall. She asked her question.

"Manwë, is this a cage?"

"No, Galadriel, it is an island, surrounded by a wide and wonderful ocean. It would take a year to walk from border to border, and there are beauties and riches that none have yet found."

"And yet there are boundaries I cannot cross."

"But why would you want to?"

"What if I did? Would you permit me?"

"Oh Galadriel, you are young yet."

"Am I a slave?"

"You are free."

"What if I wanted to go to Middle-Earth?"

"Don't go! Before you came we were so lonely."

"I didn't say I wanted to go. I was only wondering. Yes or no: if I wanted to go to Middle-Earth would you forbid it?"

"Of course you don't want to go. We have so much fun together."

Try as she might, Galadriel could not get a straight answer out of Manwë. So she turned to Yavanna, who adored Galadriel and loved to dress her up and do her hair. One day, when Yavanna was braiding her golden tresses and putting starfire in the braids, Galadriel asked her question.

Yavanna caressed her cheek. "But you mustn't go. Who will we play with? What will we do?"

"Yavanna, there's nothing more for me to learn. Manwë showed me how to make gems and gems and more gems, and I am tired of gems."

Yavanna paused in her braiding. "Stay. I'll give you a present. I'll show you how to make a mirror."

References

- Author in dispute. "Galadriel Asks The Powers." *Galadriel Apocrypha*. New York: Yavanna Publications, 288, Fifth Age.

Galadriel's Mirror

"Galadriel's Mirror" is the third of the four <u>Galadriel Apocrypha</u> texts that the Sisters of Yavanna claim to have been written by Prophet Tolkien. This claim is disputed by the <u>Church of the Elven Queen</u>.

Excerpt I

Galadriel made a mirror out of Everlasting Fire that she had sifted and sifted until it ran clear. In the mirror she saw visions. She saw herself riding an oliphaunt—a great and marvelous beast with a snake coming out of its head that lumbered along, swaying a little from side to side. She saw herself with a bow and arrow firing at a horde of invading orcs. She saw herself camping, her lovely golden tresses matted with sparkling green leaves. She saw herself cradling a baby elf—an elf she knew she had created.

She ran to Yavanna and fetched her.

"Look, Yavanna, look at what I have made!"

"These mirrors are perilous. I dare not look."

Excerpt 2

But some of the visions were terrible. One day when she and Manwë were looking into the mirror, they saw a long row of dark-skinned men and women, chains on their ankles, being marched to one of Melkor's mines.

"Is she a slave?" asked Galadriel, pointing to a small child that walked next to one of the women.

"I don't think so," said Manwë. "She hasn't got chains on. But I don't know, Galadriel. You ask such strange questions."

"I can help them," said Galadriel. "I will be a Queen! I will command the air and the water. At my touch the trees will bear fruit. Men will rally to my call, and I will lead them into battle, victorious."

"Will they be your slaves then?" asked Manwë.

Galadriel wrinkled her brow in confusion.

"No...no. I don't know." Then with greater certainty: "I won't be like that. They will follow me of their own free will."

"How can you be sure?"

Excerpt 3

Another time Yavanna was sitting with Galadriel on the marble steps, telling the story of how she had called flowers and trees and animals into being. But instead of listening, Galadriel was looking into her mirror. She saw herself among a group of South-rons, digging a mine to find gold for Melkor.

"Oh Galadriel, do pay attention!" said Yavanna.

"But look, Yavanna!"

Yavanna looked, then wrinkled her nose and grimaced and dis-taste. "Those people are dirty. Why do you even watch them?"

"But I'm one of them." Then she saw herself in a small group, huddled over a table, planning strategy for a revolt.

"Even worse," said Yavanna. "Why ever would you want to go there?"

"They're not free," said Galadriel. "Those people."

References

- Author in dispute. "Galadriel's Mirror." *Galadriel Apocrypha*. New York: Yavanna Publications, 288, Fifth Age.

Galadriel Leaves Eden

"Galadriel Leaves Eden" is the last of the four <u>Galadriel Apocrypha</u> texts that the Sisters of Yavanna claim to have been written by Prophet Tolkien. This claim is disputed by the <u>Church of the Elven Queen</u>.

This text prompted the only communication the Entfamilies have ever made. They messaged the Cyborg Sphere with seven words: "Hoom. Ah, hm, hoom. You go, Galadriel!"

Excerpt

"I know what I want," Galadriel said.

"Oh, Galadriel," said Manwë. "You can't go. You're only a child."

Galadriel laughed, deep and throaty. "I a child? No, Manwë, it is you who are the children. The Powers are the children. Watch me and learn."

References

- Author in dispute. "Galadriel Leaves Eden." *Galadriel Apocrypha*. New York: Yavanna Publications, 288, Fifth Age.

The Godmother

Mari Ness

The Godmother

The neutrality of this article may be disputed.

The Godmother, perhaps best known for interfering in the lives of <u>Cinderella</u> and <u>Prince Charming</u> and disrupting a previously happy family life and ruining the reputation of one of the most respectable matrons of the town of <u>Chauserresverre</u>.[1]

CONTENTS

Background

In the sixteenth century, the reputations of fairies were undergoing a serious decline. Infuriated by the manipulations, terrors, kidnappings, and pure screw-ups of various minor and major fairies during the <u>Middle Ages</u>, many mortals [who?] decided that they had had quite enough of fairies, thank you very much [language] and would quite simply stop believing in them, or at least stop working with them.[2]

Although fairies are not as susceptible to disbelief as is commonly believed[by whom?] [weasel words] this decision sent many of the fairies and <u>fairy kingdoms</u> into a panic. Among these was the fairy later identified only as The Godmother, whose kindly countenance concealed one of the most ruthless minds to be found in any of the fairy kingdoms.

Her precise identity is uncertain, although certainly her chosen appearance as a kindly old lady was and remains merely an illusion put on for the occasion and to hide her true motivations; fairies of her power can invariably make themselves beautiful. Some scholars [who?] suggest that she may have been one of <u>Morgan le Fay</u>'s main ladies-in-waiting; others suggest that she was no more than a low born sprite, perhaps of no parentage whatsoever—literally of no parentage whatsoever—who hoped that her machinations would earn her a place among fairy royalty.

In any case, she decided to stage an event that would swing sympathies back to the fairies, setting up the story of Cinderella.[3]

Cinderella

Prior to the interference of the Godmother, documentary evidence suggests that Cinderella—then known by her formal name of Ella Marie Christine d'Epant—in fact enjoyed a relatively warm and loving family life, first with her beloved mother and father, and later with her father's second wife, a woman from a solid, respectable merchant's family, living a comfortable existence in the town of Chauserresverre. Family letters suggest that although Ella endured the typical sibling rivalry with her elder stepsister, Madeleine, she was on closer terms with her second stepsister, Charlotte, and found the presence of stepmother and sisters a great comfort upon the death of her father.[4] But a comfortable, indeed banal, family environment provides little room for fairy workings. [5] Accordingly, the Godmother, noting Ella's singular beauty and realizing that her geographical proximity and relatively respectable birth allowed her the opportunity to make a match with a very minor prince if the conditions were properly set, cast a spell upon Ella's stepmother. The results were immediate; the stepmother underwent a personality change that quite shocked neighbors and servants alike, ordering Ella to do the most menial of household tasks without assistance.

Some evidence suggests that Ella's stepsisters initially offered assistance, in a far cry from their unsympathetic portrayal in other accounts. In any case, all agree that Ella soon found herself covered in dirt and soot, a grotesque and pitiful figure, earning her better-known nickname of Cinderella. Ella reacted in typical teenage fashion, rebelling and refusing orders; upon seeing this, the

Godmother waved a wand, transforming Ella into a nearly unbelievable model of obedience and honesty.[6]

That set up, the Godmother then switched to the next stage of her plan. Chauserresverre was at the time ruled by a very minor noble family who had just raised themselves to princely status. Desperate for increased influence, they had planned to use their new, if somewhat questionable, titles to marry their younger son to a wealthy noblewoman, perhaps even a princess. The town's mayor, hearing of the plan, said in response, "Charming." This dry rejoinder was soon attached as a nickname to the young supposed prince.

The Godmother had few difficulties in creating obstacles to stand in the way of this proposed marriage, or of creating a quiet suggestion that the very best thing his parents could do would be to throw a ball, demonstrating the prince's desirability as a marriage partner. Charming's parents agreed enthusiastically, and so the stage was set.

On the night of the ball, the Godmother twisted the enchantment on Cinderella's stepmother to make the poor woman even more cruel; then, when the house was deserted and stepmother and sisters were on the way to the ball, entered the kitchen. The next few minutes were filled with acts of terrible torture and animal cruelty, as several mice found themselves stretching to the size of horses, a rat found himself forced, for the first time, to walk upright, an activity that left him bruised and shaking since he had never attempted anything like this, and Cinderella herself was squeezed into a hideous corset and bodice, which made breathing impossible, and forced to walk in delicate glass shoes that could easily shatter and slice through her feet with a single wrong step. Even the vegetation of the household were not spared, as a prize pumpkin was transformed to a rather slow and nearly useless carriage.

The trauma almost proved too much for poor Cinderella, the mice, and the rats, but the Godmother insisted: under the terrible force of her wand the group trundled to the palace, where the terrified

Cinderella slowly climbed the steps in constant fear of cutting her feet.[7]

Fortunately for the success of the Godmother's plan, Charming was terrified of the women at the ball and headed out to the steps to try to calm his mind. The mutual terror of Charming and Cinderella made an instant bond, and after one painful, awkward, dance, they headed out to the gardens to get to know each other a little better. Things went so well, indeed, that Cinderella almost forgot the Godmother's strict instructions, nearly ruining the entire plan by staying until the very stroke of midnight.

The watching Godmother was only able to save her plan by a small trick of the wand that pulled the glass slipper from Cinderella's foot, leaving it on the steps. Charming, finding this shoe moments later, decided to track down the owner of the slipper, and the rest was a triumph for the Godmother's story, if not for the poor stepmother, who suffered cruel torments for the rest of her days.[8]

Aftermath

The Godmother's actions were not universally praised by her fellow fairies, who were appalled by the Godmother's manipulations of human emotions. They therefore banished the Godmother for some time from mortal lands, particularly from christenings, although this latter gesture did little to save other young princesses unfortunate enough to encounter fairies. The Godmother was forced to save her reputation through writing lengthy screeds to various chroniclers of fairy histories. Some of these screeds so annoyed their recipients that they went to great lengths to remove her from retellings of the Cinderella tale.[9] Other annoyed recipients assured readers that fairies were not real, or that they were deeply wicked, or that they were often old and ugly—versions of the tale guaranteed to irk the Godmother.[10]

An infuriated Godmother began to take cold revenge. Writers of fairy tales unwilling to honor the Godmother and other fairies—or portray them in a manner the Godmother deemed acceptable—

soon found their lives turning into unsinkable horrors, attacked by small fairies, talking cats, singing harps that could not be quieted, cruel stepparents, and, worst of all, indestructible obstacles to true love. Several horrified chroniclers even found dead pets in their beds. Although some—notably the Grimms—remained strong, still refusing to feature the Godmother in their histories, others quickly capitulated. By the late nineteenth century, a terrified Andrew Lang was granting her a prominent role and the right to approve all illustrations in her retellings.[11]

The Godmother was also linked to other incidents of cruelty and manipulation throughout the nineteenth and early twentieth centuries, and is widely regarded among experts as one of the most dangerous of the fairies, whatever her kindly demeanor. By the mid-twentieth century, Disney animators, mindful of the legends, were careful to portray her and other fairies in a purely benevolent manner.[12]

The Godmother's current whereabouts are a matter of some dispute. She is believed by some to be working in a Wall Street Bank and by others to be blackmailing several major Hollywood studios and publishing houses.[13]

Notes/References

1   Perrault, Charles. *Histories ou contes du temps passé.* Paris, 1697; *The Complete Fairy Tales in Verse and Prose: A Dual Language Book.* Edited and translated by Stanley Applebaum. Mineola, New York: Dover, 2002; Lang, Andrew. *The Blue Fairy Book.* New York: Dover, 1965.

2   Dormir, Adele Lanyon, *Fairies: The Untold Economic Destruction.* Glastonbury: Orfeo Chevalier and Co. Ltd., 2004; Hawthorne, Goldilocks. *Gangsters in Fairy Kingdoms.* Twilight Springs: If We Swear Up and Down That We're Really Mundane, Will You Believe Us PLEASE Books, 2010.

3   Perrault, Charles. *Histories ou contes du temps passé.* Paris, 1697; *The Complete Fairy Tales in Verse and Prose: A Dual

Language Book. Edited and translated by Stanley Applebaum. Mineola, New York: Dover, 2002.

4 Ibid.

5 D'Aulnoy, Marie Catherine Baronne. *Court Politics in Enchanted Kingdoms.* Nuages: Impossiblé Presse de France, 1892.

6 Perrault, Charles. *Histories ou contes du temps passé.* Paris, 1697; *The Complete Fairy Tales in Verse and Prose: A Dual Language Book.* Edited and translated by Stanley Applebaum. Mineola, New York: Dover, 2002; Lang, Andrew. *The Blue Fairy Book.* New York: Dover, 1965; Grimm, Jacob and Wilhelm. *Children's and Household Tales.* Berlin, 1812-1815.

7 Perrault, Charles. *Histories ou contes du temps passé.* Paris, 1697; *The Complete Fairy Tales in Verse and Prose: A Dual Language Book.* Edited and translated by Stanley Applebaum. Mineola, New York: Dover, 2002; Hawthorne, Goldilocks. *Gangsters in Fairy Kingdoms.* Twilight Springs: If We Swear Up and Down That We're Really Mundane, Will You Believe Us PLEASE Books, 2010.

8 Grimm, Jacob and Wilhelm. *Children's and Household Tales.* Berlin, 1812-1815; Perrault, Charles. *Histories ou contes du temps passé.* Paris, 1697; *The Complete Fairy Tales in Verse and Prose: A Dual Language Book.* Edited and translated by Stanley Applebaum. Mineola, New York: Dover, 2002; d'Epant, Madame, *Memoirs*, manuscript in the collection of the Scholae of Avalon, 16th century.

9 Grimm, Jacob and Wilhelm. *Children's and Household Tales.* Berlin, 1812-1815; Lang, Andrew, *The Fairy Tale Books*, Mineola, New York: Dover: 1965-1968.

10 D'Aulnoy, Marie Catherine Baronne. *Court Politics in Enchanted Kingdoms.* Nuages: Impossiblé Presse de France, 1892.

11 Grimm, Jacob and Wilhelm. *Children's and Household Tales.* Berlin, 1812-1815; Lang, Andrew, *The Fairy Tale Books*, Mineola, New York: Dover: 1965-1968.

12 Thomas, Mickey, "Fairies and Theme Parks: An Insider's Eye," Nonestica: Red Queen Press, 2007.

13 Citation removed by unknown source.

Marmalette

Mari Ness

Marmalette

Marmalette, the second fairy to grant a magical gift at the christening of <u>Aurora d'Belle Roses d'Fantastique</u>, was widely criticized for her role in this and many previous and subsequent disasters with minor members of the European nobility.[1]

CONTENTS

Early Life and Seductions

Marmalette's birthplace remains a matter of some dispute. She has been variously said to have been born "somewhere in France," on <u>the back of the West Wind</u>, upon the Isle of <u>Avalon</u>, on the back of a dragon, and inside a rosebud in an undisclosed location. Some historians [who?] have claimed that the discrepancies in these birthplaces are nothing more than a pathetic attempt to escape taxation [weasel words].

Her first confirmed appearance was in <u>Languedoc</u>, in the early twelfth century, where she rang bells to save virgin princesses [clarification needed], although some stories place her in <u>Spain</u> in the eighth century, a country she fled upon the arrival of the Arabs, who brought new fairies hostile to the resident supernatural population [dubious — discuss]. In Languedoc she began what was then the normal training regimen for young French fairies of good blood—and by fairy standards, Marmalette was quite young—seducing young knights planning to head off to the <u>Crusades</u>.

Although this was undoubtedly done to increase her standing in fairy courts,[2] Marmalette was later quoted as saying that this was for charitable purposes, since although the knights she seduced spent (some say wasted) many years in fairy captivity, they at least avoided the horror of the Crusades and ate exceedingly well in the meantime.

As the Crusades waned, however, Marmalette seems to have decided that continuous seducing of young, not always well-favored knights was growing progressively dull. She applied for and received a position as Fairy Godmother, although due to her lack of experience, she was continually placed in secondary roles as a backup fairy at christenings.

Fairy Godmothering

For the next few hundred years, Marmalette attended a number of christenings in the European area. (Allegations that she also attended and disrupted multiple christenings in the Middle East have been widely discredited, mostly because the Middle East does not have many christenings, although the terrible fates that oppressed <u>Aladdin</u> and other figures of that geographical area do suggest her inept meddling.) Without fail, each and every christening she attended had disastrous results.[3]

At least one queen [who?] was heard to sob that she wished Marmalette would go back to seducing knights—at least it would rid the palace of some unnecessary, good-looking men who were taking far too much interest in various clever goose girls.

Some of her recent defenders have said that this was not limited to Marmalette, and that any christening attended by fairies invariably led to disaster. Indeed, at least some historians have blamed the general political instability of the fourteenth through seventeenth centuries on the seeming inability of European nobility and royalty to stop inviting fairies to their christenings.[4]

Nonetheless, Marmalette was connected to particularly problematic incidents, and in the early seventeenth century she seems to have taken a brief pause in the christening business to improve her party skills.

Sleeping Beauty

In 1647, Marmalette unexpectedly received yet another invitation to a royal christening, of <u>Aurora d'Belle Roses</u>, who had been born somewhat unexpectedly to a minor, previously believed infertile, king and queen of a small country called Carnationodoc. The christening was expected to create some political challenges, since other heirs had expected to vie for the tiny kingdom. Thus, the seven fairies were invited, less for their gifts and more in the hopes of providing distraction. (This last helps explain why the older fairies were not invited—their angry visages could not have added much to diplomacy.)[5]

The exact gift granted by Marmalette is in some dispute. At least one account appears to claim that Marmalette gave the baby princess the "wit of an angel," but he has been found to be inaccurate in many accounts,[6] and it must be confessed that the young princess, then or later, was never seen to display much wit, angelic or otherwise.[citation needed] In other accounts, the princess received the ability to dance, which, as several have noted, would have been part of her standard training as a princess and aristocrat, and thus as fairy gifts go, seems rather meager.

Regardless, all chroniclers agree that Marmalette had already granted her gift, and was therefore powerless to intervene when an eighth, uninvited fairy showed up, casting a spell upon the baby princess. In some accounts, Marmalette argued fiercely against the ban on spinning wheels that then followed; in other accounts, this ban came at her suggestion.

On the princess's sixteenth birthday, she encountered a spinning wheel and passed out from the shock.[7] All living things in the building with her, including her parents, the king and queen, fell asleep at precisely that moment. Marmalette was by most accounts nowhere near the palace, having completely forgotten the date. (In one disputed account she helped send the rest of the palace into its enchanted sleep.) With her abilities to transport humans from one place to another, and her reported ownership of seven league boots, Marmalette was later widely criticized, along with the other original fairies, for not removing at least some administrative and military personnel from the palace just prior to the birthday celebrations.

Financial Collapse

The sudden inaccessibility of the king, queen, and senior members of the royal household sent the kingdom into sudden turmoil and disarray. Hearing of this, three nearby kingdoms immediately invaded, sending the kingdom into still further misery and sorrow. Conservative estimates suggest that perhaps a full fourth of the population died within the first ten years, with another fourth fleeing to France, spreading tales of the destruction as they fled. Multiple minor princes, sensing the opportunity to gain a kingdom at comparatively little cost, also assaulted the area, heading straight for the doomed palace, but soon found themselves caught and killed by angry peasants and rosebushes. The resulting massacre "doomed a generation of the flower of royalty," and if some felt that Europe was better off with fewer princes, the ferocity and greed of the remaining ones did not provide much comfort.[8]

Sexual Scandal

About one hundred years after the Great Pricking, the Palace d'Aurore suddenly emerged from the vines that had enclosed it, with no real explanation given. Its wrecked and ruined prisoners slowly crept from the palace, clutching whatever gems could be salvaged from the mess, spreading tales of the horror of their captivity as they went.

Among these tales was the report that the princess, while in enchanted sleep, had been ravished [emotional language?] by at least one and possibly several princes, giving birth to at least two children. Since the palace had been cut off from all outside visitors for that period, it was immediately realized that the prince or princes could only have been brought into the palace with the assistance of fairies.

Suspicion immediately turned to Marmalette, with her history of seducing knights and her teleportation abilities. She immediately denied all such reports, but these, along with the complete wreckage of the kingdom and her prior disasters at christening, were enough to cause her a temporary banishment from the fairy courts and a decided decline in prestige.[9]

Later Years

As the popularity of fairy attendance at christenings waned (no doubt because of the myriad disasters associated with these events, whatever their eventual happy endings), Marmalette found herself out of a job. She was next reported in <u>Paris</u> salons, telling her tearful story to women, a role that gained her some advocates but also generated still more criticism.

After the <u>French Revolution</u> closed most of the <u>Paris</u> salons, particularly the ones that had delighted in elaborate oral storytelling, Marmalette found herself relegated more and more to jobs overseeing children, although even here she often found difficulty gaining employment, since many <u>Victorian</u> parents were wary of fairy influence upon children. By the time the twentieth century rolled around, Marmalette had faded into perhaps welcome obscurity.

The Disney Controversy

In the early 1950s, the Walt Disney Company decided to make a film based on the Sleeping Beauty incident, featuring seven fairies as a sort of mirror to the popular seven dwarfs of their earlier film,

Snow White.[10] Justly concerned that the film would paint her in a negative light, Marmalette, accompanied by two of the other fairies from that infamous christening, rushed to California to do extensive damage control.

Nonetheless, Walt Disney did not take kindly to the interference and ordered his artists to portray the three good fairies as elderly women in simple gowns, instead of the somewhat more realistic if also only slightly clothed fairies he had shown in *Fantasia*.

Since the film's original appearance, Marmalette has again mostly faded into obscurity, although *The Fae Bulletin* reported that she and other fairies are considering suing Disney for a percentage of the merchandising revenue for Disney's Princess line.[11]

Notes/References

1 Dormir, Adele Lanyon, *Fairies: The Untold Economic Destruction*. Glastonbury: Orfeo Chevalier and Co. Ltd., 2004; France, Anatole, *Secret Histories*. Paris: Calaman-Levy, 1908; Lang, Andrew. *The Blue Fairy Book*. New York: Dover, 1965; Perrault, Charles. *Histories ou contes du temps passé*. Paris, 1697; Perrault, Charles. *The Complete Fairy Tales in Verse and Prose: A Dual Language Book*. Edited and translated by Stanley Applebaum. Mineola, New York: Dover, 2002.

2 D'Aulnoy, Marie Catherine Baronne.*Court Politics in Enchanted Kingdoms*. Nuages: Impossiblé Presse de France, 1892.

3 D'Aulnoy, Marie Catherine Baronne.*Court Politics in Enchanted Kingdoms*. Nuages: Impossiblé Presse de France, 1892; Perrault, Charles. *The Complete Fairy Tales in Verse and Prose: A Dual Language Book*. Edited and translated by Stanley Applebaum. Mineola, New York: Dover, 2002; Glas-Foraoise, Mazoe: *A Dictionary of Supernatural Biographies: Europe*. Avalon: Green Knight Press, 1989.

4 Roobin-Hood, T.D., *Christenings and Catalysms: Fairy Interference with the Economic Development of Western*

Europe and the Modern Nation State, Nuages: Universite de Enchantee Press, 2008.

5 Perrault, Charles. *Histories ou contes du temps passé.* Paris, 1697; Perrault, Charles. *The Complete Fairy Tales in Verse and Prose: A Dual Language Book.* Edited and translated by Stanley Applebaum. Mineola, New York: Dover, 2002.

6 Zipes, Jack, *Beauties, Beasts, and Enchantment: Classic French Fairy Tales, translated with an introduction on "The Rise of the French Fairy Tale and the Decline of France,"* New York: New American Library, 1989.

7 Anonymous. *A Lady Remembers: Visits to the Courts of France and Italy in Twilight.* Avalon: Twilight Star Press, 1984; Rooobin-Hood, T.D., *Prestige and Economics in the Fairy Courts of Western Europe.* Nuages: Universite de Enchantee Press, 1992.

8 Roobin-Hood, T.D., *Christenings and Catalysms: Fairy Interference with the Economic Development of Western Europe and the Modern Nation State,* Nuages: Universite de Enchantee Press, 2008; Glas-Foraoise, Mazoe, *A General History of Enchantments,* Avalon: Excalibur Press, 1885; 2nd edition 1953; 3rd edition 1996.

9 D'Aulnoy, Marie Catherine Baronne.*Court Politics in Enchanted Kingdoms.* Nuages: Impossiblé Presse de France, 1892.

10 We aren't allowed to tell you our source on this, but the initials have something to do with the letter "M."

11 Ravagio, Tourmentine, "Mortals May Not Believe in Fairies, But They Believe in Their Revenue," *The Fae Bulletin,* May 1, 2012.

See Also

- Mother Holle
- Scholae of Avalon
- Christening dangers
- Crusades
- Fairy godmothers

Palatina

Mari Ness

Palatina

Princess Palatina of Albany, daughter of Elynas of Albany and Pressina (sometimes called Pressyne) of Avalon, princess of Scotland, sister of Melusine of Poitou, famous for betraying her father and subsequently being forced to guard his treasure. [1]

Genealogy

Palatina was the second daughter of Elynas of Albany, himself a direct descendant of no less than three Trojan heroes and thus—illegitimately and illicitly—of direct divine parentage.[2] These advantages of birth apparently inspired his decision to style himself the rightful king of the Scots, even though he inherited and controlled at most one small castle and a second manor in Scotland. To bolster his claim, Elynas decided to seek out a fairy wife. Unfortunately, his lack of wealth made him unattractive to all but the most desperate of fairy brides.[3]

His wife's origins are shrouded in mystery: even the spelling of her name is in doubt, with some chroniclers [who?] spelling it as Pressina, and others Pressyne, and still others Presto. She may have been one of the attendants of Morgan le Fay, although she does not appear in any reliable court lists from Avalon at that period. Others [who?] have theorized that she sprang up from a mushroom, [citation needed] and, considering that enough qualification for fairy blood, hunted down a human noble to provide her some respectability. This theory is disputed by those [who?] who believe that fairies can never be respectable, or, contrarywise, are respectable merely by being fairies.

Nevertheless, Pressina was enough of a fairy to attract Elynas, and although it is well known that alliances between fairies and mortals with divine blood may produce unfortunate results, the two married at some time in the eighth century. In accordance with then-fairy law, Pressina set magical conditions upon their marriage. Naturally, these conditions were soon violated, and Pressina set off to Avalon, with three daughters in tow.[4]

Training in Avalon and Revenge

Palatina and her two sisters—the older Melusine and the younger Melias—received an exquisite training in magical arts and fairy courtesies and manners under the tutelage of Morgan le Fay. When not at lessons, however, the three frequently conspired together to enact revenge against their father for his supposed ill treatment of his father.

The sisters kept these plans from their mother, however, and Palatina, with her intelligence and steady purpose, rapidly became a favorite of their mother, which doubtless explains why her punishment was—at least on the surface—less severe than those of her sisters.

The punishment came swiftly enough. As soon as they had learned sufficient magic from Morgan le Fay, the sisters imprisoned their father in a mine, and worse, imprisoned him in an _English_ mine. Pressina reacted quickly, cursing all three of her daughters in return.[5]

Cursed, the Early Years

Pressina's gaze softened, however, when she looked at her second, favorite daughter, and the conditions of Palatina's curse seem mild enough. She was to guard her father's treasure until a descendant of her sister Melusine came to free it. For a half-fairy with her training, guarding and hiding a treasure—any treasure—was simple enough, and indeed took so little effort that Palatina had plenty of time to curl up with impossible tales of fairy romances.[6]

Unfortunately, these conditions failed to take into account just one tiny detail: the treasure of Elynas was simply not worth seeking out.

Elynas had been a poverty-stricken king to begin with, and most of his treasure had gone to wooing and wedding his wife. Left were three copper bowls, none in particularly good shape, one bronze pin, and a poorly carved statue that might have been of Venus and of Roman origin—Elynas certainly thought so—but which even the very few art experts of 8th century Britain correctly identified as more probably the work of a very small child. So poor indeed was the treasure that even local dragons, hearing of it, declined the mere thought of adding it to their hordes.

Adding to the problem: although Melusine, out of love and kindness for her trapped sister, hastily bedded her handsome husband as frequently as possible, she, too, was cursed with fairy magic. Her marriage did not last long. Thanks to the curse, her children were all hideously, hideously ugly, and thanks to the poor family history of marriage, some were even inclined to seek the safe chastity of nearby monasteries. (By all accounts, the monasteries were not pleased to welcome them, but softened with the application of fairy gold.) Pressina did what she could to improve their beauty and charm, but at that distance (Melusine had moved to France, and the treasure, such as it wasn't, was still in Scotland) her spells were of only limited use.

The inevitable happened: only two of Melusine's sons managed to have children at all. A desperate Pressina pleaded with her sister to marry a second time, but this was impossible: Melusine had gained a permanent tail that magically covered up some of the most necessary organs for the creation of children. Melusine's few descendants, warned of the limited treasure that awaited them in Scotland should they chose to claim it, headed for the Crusades instead.[7]

Although some contemporary nobles and pretenders continue to claim Melusine as an ancestor, the descendants of Melusine died out by the seventh generation. Palatina was trapped.

Interference in Later Scottish History

A bored Palatina is accused of spending the next several centuries working to weaken and topple Scottish monarchs in vengeful fury at the country whose eighth-century poverty had left her so trapped. Scottish monarchs allegedly harmed by her spells include Kings Donnchad and his successor, Mac Bethad, although some historians prefer to blame their troubles on the interference of irritated witches and talking trees.[8] She is most plausibly blamed for the many mishaps of Mary Queen of Scots, using her fairy spells to cause the doomed queen to fall hopelessly in love first with the feckless Henry Stuart, Lord Darnley, and later with the even less suitable Earl of Bothwell, using a powerful if short-lived enchantment. [citation needed] This final interference helped to doom the independency of the Scottish crown [dubious — discuss], and although James VI and I and his successors continued to make regular visits to Scotland, they remained largely out of Palatina's reach. Lacking even the ability to take petty revenge, she consoled herself with writing irritated letters to her sister, Melusine, who, after reading them, sent these missives out into the wind and the rain.[9]

Palatina currently resides in a small cottage overlooking the cave that holds her father's tiny treasure. She is reported to be considering setting up a small museum and a tea shop to gain the income she needs to enter the new electronic world.

Notes/References

1   d'Arras, Jean, *Chronique de Melusine, Le Noble Hystoire de Lusigan*, multiple manuscripts, approximately 1393.

2   Homer, *The Iliad;* Virgil, *The Aeneid*; Mostopho Aranyas, *A Genealogy of the Trojans and the Royal Courts of Europe, with some Unfortunate Illustrations,* Nonestica: Red Queen Press, 1902; Glas-Foraoise, Mazoe. *A Genealogy of Some Noted Persons of Noble Fairy Blood*. Avalon: Excalibur Press, 1954.

3   Harper, Jonas, *"Prithee, Dear Knight,"* Sexual Conquest and Enchantments in Fairy Courts in the early Middle Ages, Avalon: Whispering Wind Press, 1994.

4   d'Arras, Jean, *Chronique de Melusine, Le Noble Hystoire de Lusigan*, multiple manuscripts, approximately 1393.

5   d'Arras, Jean, *Chronique de Melusine, Le Noble Hystoire de Lusigan*, multiple manuscripts, approximately 1393; Orkney, Sir Agravaine, *The Shadows of Avalon: A Memoir*, Glastonbury: Orfeo Chevalier Co., 1954.

6   d'Arras, Jean, *Chronique de Melusine, Le Noble Hystoire de Lusigan*, multiple manuscripts, approximately 1393; Ablach, Tyronoe, *Fairies: A Less Poetic Approach*, Avalon: Green Knight Press, 1912.

7   *I Cannot Take Any More of These Dying Birds and Mournful Songs: The Collected Correspondence of Marguerite-Amelie d'Seductrice-Levres, La Belle Dame Sans Merci* ed Orfeo Chevalier, Avalon: Green Knight Press, 1938, revised edition 1996; Orkney, Agrivaine, Sir, le Noir, Bruner, Sir, Bouffon, Dagonet, Baron; *Historiae Harleiae (400-1400)* Avalon: Excalibur Press, 1923; Dormir, Adele Lanyon, *Fairies: The Untold Economic Destruction*. Glastonbury: Orfeo Chevalier and Co. Ltd., 2004; Glas-Foraoise, Mazoe: *A Dictionary of Supernatural Biographies: Europe*. Avalon: Green Knight Press, 1989.

8   Shakespeare, William, *Macbeth*. G. Blakemore Evans (ed.), in *The Riverside Shakespeare*. Boston: Houghton Mifflin

Company, 1974; Tolkien, J.R.R. *The Ents Did It: a study of the political forces literally raised by the walking trees of Scotland,* manuscript in private collection and very carefully guarded, but copied on mushrooms, probable date of 1972.

9   d'Lusignan, Melusine, *Fairy Courtesies: a Memoir of More Modern Times.* Avalon: Green Knight Press, 1965.

The Blacksmith

Catherine Krahe

The Blacksmith

This article refers to the European craftsman. For other uses, see Blacksmith (disambiguation).

The Blacksmith (c. 1500), birth name unknown, was a famed ironworker known for his long and irregular career and unique metal footwear. He is known to have lived in both the Northern City and the City of the Forest, but spent the majority of his life near the Glass Mountain. His work can be found in museums run by the Northern Kingdom and the University of the Forest, as well as regional museums and private collections.

CONTENTS

Early Life and Apprenticeship

The Blacksmith was born in the Northern City about two decades before the coronation of the Gosling Queen. He was the youngest son of a shoemaker and left his family at a young age to apprentice to a blacksmith. Little else is known about his family life.[1] He is said to have been very tall, with the strength of three men, and able to work for hours.[2]

He first rose to prominence during the coronation of the Gosling Queen. The dispossessed queen had met him after the death of her horse Falaba, and it is thought that he was the man who nailed the stallion's head above the castle gate.[1] The queen's memoirs mention, "a man of unusual size yet gentle mien whose great strength lifted brave Falaba easily. I have been much comforted by his presence and support."[2,3] Six months later, when the false queen was revealed, the Gosling Queen called upon the Blacksmith to make five hundred long, sharp nails, which were then driven into the famed <u>barrel</u> used to execute her.[3] The Blacksmith was to be given a gold cup studded with sapphires during the coronation feast, but vanished some time before the coronation proper.[3] Some researchers think that the Blacksmith's move to the Glass Mountain was to avoid repercussions from a romantic relationship with the Queen, but this has been largely discredited because he did nothing to hide himself or his trail.[2,4]

The Glass Mountain Years

The Blacksmith left the North Kingdom after the Gosling Queen's coronation. He made his way slowly through the towns and villages and does not seem to have been recognized.[4]

Between two and four years later, the Blacksmith is known to have settled near the foot of the Glass Mountain to the west of the North Kingdom. The exact location of his home is unknown, but is thought to be near the village of <u>Slopeheim</u> in the eastern silicate foothills. This was a very odd choice for a blacksmith as the area is only sparsely settled. He stayed there for almost the entire rest of his life.[1]

The Blacksmith's domestic period is not well documented. The church records in Slopeheim are incomplete due to <u>flash floods</u> off the mountain. One entry is of a marriage between the Blacksmith and a "traveling woman" here taken to mean a woman not born in the village. A bit more than seven years later, a traveling woman's funeral is held, presumably the Blacksmith's wife. Women's lives were harder in those times, and many died in childbirth. No baptisms are recorded to any of the couples thought to be the Blacksmith, though, and since excavation of the churchyard has not revealed graves likely to belong to the wife of a prominent and prolific craftsman, it is much more likely that the Blacksmith lived alone during this period.[citation needed] He probably needed a break after the Gosling Queen.

The Glass Mountain years were not a fallow period, however. It was during this time that the Blacksmith returned to his cobbler's roots and pioneered iron shoes. Few examples of his initial designs have survived, but it is clear that they began as hobnailed boots. Later designs anchored the cleats in a solid sole, but modern reconstructions have shown that this is very difficult to walk in. Since the shoes were specifically for scaling the Glass Mountain, this was unsuitable. The hinged sole came next, but it was years before the Blacksmith developed the glass-clinging multiply-hinged sole that now characterizes his work. The sole can bend at each toe, the ball of the foot, and the heel. Iron spikes set in the sole dig into the surface and enable the wearer to climb even the most forbidding slope of the Glass Mountain.[5]

The Blacksmith continued refining the iron shoes over the next two and a half decades, but did not significantly change them. Most of the new shoes are more elegant and may have been sold to adventurers and pleasure climbers.

Return to Prominence

The Blacksmith had essentially disappeared from popular thought while he lived at the Glass Mountain. However, he was still known among craftsmen for the iron shoes. Before the wedding of the Snow-White Queen in the City of the Forest, he was called upon to make another pair. The Smith's Guild of the City of the Forest objected, but the order had come from the Royal Castle itself. The Prince and then-Princess may have known about the Blacksmith from communication with the Northern City and decided he would be a fit executioner for her mother, the Jealous Queen. Some scholars believe that by commissioning a human craftsman rather than continuing the Snow-White Princess's ties to the dwarves, this wedding caused the Second Dwarf War.[citation needed]

The shoes the Blacksmith made in the City of the Forest were his last. They can still be found in the University of the Forest's collections. They look very different from the mountain-climbing shoes the Blacksmith normally forged, but the hinged sole remains. However, they are essentially iron knee-boots with clasps around the calves.[6] The Blacksmith was so offended by the account of the Snow-White Queen that he added needles to the boots, which would have made dancing even more painful and echo the five hundred iron nails he made in the Northern City.[citation needed] One hypothesis is that the spikes held some sort of liquid, which would have been injected into the Jealous Queen's calves as she 'danced' during her execution, but chemical analysis in 2007 revealed only traces of glucose, fructose, other sugars, and malic acid, found in apple juice and other fruits.[6] Contemporary accounts say that the Queen gave "a great and long scream as the shoes were buckled, and cried, 'What have you done to me?'" She then moved her arms as if dancing a Glass Mountain estampie for no more than a minute before falling still.[7] This is not in keeping with modern reconstructions of the execution because burning, even via shoes, is a gruesome, painful death. It is very unlikely that she actually died so quickly from the pain alone.[6]

The Blacksmith did not stay in the City of the Forest very long. One report of the execution mentions a tall, broad man past the prime of life who watched until the Queen died, then bowed his head and turned away.[7] This is consistent with the Blacksmith's distaste for executions and city life in general. Again, he was to be honored at the wedding feast, this time with a medal, but he never arrived.

Artifacts

Many of the Blacksmith's shoes can be found in museums. The barrel that killed the False Queen was displayed on the castle gates, where Falaba's head had hung, but was destroyed in a storm fifty-eight years later. Nearly four hundred of the nails were recovered and can be seen during tours of the Northern City's Tower of Jewels. Counterfeits abound and should not be trusted.[citation needed]

The <u>Glass Mountain Museum</u> has collected seventeen pairs of shoes clearly showing the design process. Eight of them are on display.

The University of the Forest holds two pairs of the Blacksmith's shoes, the deadly knee-boots and a pair of the Blacksmith's iron shoes with glass-clinging soles, thought to be the earliest of that design and to have once belonged to the Jealous Queen.

Notes/References

1   March, Jared. *Lives of Common Figures*. New York: Dover Thrift Editions, 2000.

2   "Ten Badass Men You Never Learned About in School" <u>cracked.com</u>, June 18, 2010.

3   Eicherberger and White, *Memoirs of the Royal Family of the North Kingdom*. London: Oxford University Press, 1955.

4   Liang, Brandt, and Mendoza. "Following the iron shoes: an investigation into the Blacksmith and his travels." <u>*International Journal of Historical Archaeology*</u>, vol 12, 2009.

5   Liang, Tina. "Initial designs of the iron shoe: purpose, experimentation, and genius." 2008 Conference on Historical and Underwater Archaeology.

6   Hartman, Liang, and Mendoza. "Deadly design: was the red-hot shoe an efficient method of execution?" *International Journal of Historical Archaeology*, vol 10, 2007.

7   *Five Years in the Forest City, A Lady of Quality*. New York: Dover Thrift Editions, 1998.

Peter Rabbit

Jenni Moody

Peter Rabbit

From Bunnypedia, the free encyclopedia

*For the article on the musical group, see **Peter and the Rabbits***

Peter Rabbit (1900-1912) was an English country florist renowned for his cabbage and for founding *Planned Rabbithood*, a non-profit organization that provsides free reproductive education. He was the brother of the acclaimed memoirist Flopsy Bunny. Peter appears as the protagonist in *The Tale of Peter Rabbit*, the most popular volume in Flopsy Bunny's *Life in the Garden* series.

CONTENTS
1 Early Life
2 Public Reception
3 Controversy
4 Later Life
5 Recent Developments
5 Notes/References

Early Life

In interviews conducted with Peter's sisters Mopsy and Cotton-tail after the publication of *The Tale of Peter Rabbit*, they described the life of the young rabbit as troubled. "After our father disappeared, Peter began to hang out with the wrong crowd. He would come in late at night with cuts in his clothing and heads of lettuce for us to eat."[1]

A special report by RBBT 42 news anchor Amami Oshima explored the strong connection between Peter Rabbit and his father. Archival footage of the interview shows Oshima sitting on the family sofa with Mrs. Josephine Rabbit as they look through a photo album together. "They were inseparable," Mrs. Rabbit said as she flipped the pages in the scrapbook. She rested her paw on the corner of a photograph of Peter riding on his father's back. "Peter came back that day from Mr. McGregor's garden in shock. He couldn't even cry or tell us what had happened. All he would say was that his father was gone."[2] Promotional materials for the special report showed the now famous photograph of Peter and his father gardening together, dressed in matching coveralls.[3]

Public Reception

When published, _The Tale of Peter Rabbit_ was hailed as an extraordinary portrayal of the journey of a troubled young rabbit teen from a life of crime to a life based on family values. Sales of the book tripled overnight, after _The Lagomorph Times_ printed a book review by famed rabbitorial senator Mo Glire. "As I read this tale," Glire stated, "I saw in it the journey so many of our young rabbitmen make these days. From the dangerous life of theft, to the comforts of family. It is my recommendation that _The Tale of Peter Rabbit_ be read by every mother to her litter-ones."[4]

In a 1907 poll, 83% of new mothers said that they read _The Tale of Peter Rabbit_ to their children every night, followed by admonitions about their own local farmers' gardens. An additional 15% admitted to reading the book to their brood once a week, and the remaining 2% said that they had suspended regular reading of the story to their young ones due to the terrifying nature of the story. These in the last category acknowledged that they kept the book in a prominent position over the fireplace, and threatened to take it down and read it whenever their children were suspected of stealing produce.[5]

Controversy

As the fame of _The Tale of Peter Rabbit_ grew, Peter Rabbit himself became an increasingly public figure. He often accompanied his sister on her book tours. Local papers from 1907-1909 show an average of one photograph per issue of Peter Rabbit with a kit in his arms, often with his paw playfully wagging in front of the newborn's nose, as if to warn the child of the dangers of garden robbery.[6]

In 1910, Peter Rabbit again made front page news. A photograph from *The Meadow Gazette* showed local firefighters cutting Peter down from a nail on the outside of Mr. McGregor's fence. A half-eaten head of lettuce was on the ground nearby.[7] Peter suffered multiple fracture wounds and was transported to Mercy Hospital, where he made a full recovery.[citation needed]

Following news of Peter Rabbit's attempted theft, Flopsy Bunny's publisher discontinued her book tour. Sales of *The Tale of Peter Rabbit* flagged,[8] and local newspapers immediately discontinued stories of Peter's visits to local schools and nurseries.[9]

Later Life

After the incident at McGregor's garden, Peter retreated from public life. His sisters helped him run a small florist shop, and in his last years he founded *Planned Rabbithood*, a non-profit organization that provides reproductive education and counseling services.[10]

Peter Rabbit passed away in 1912 after a fourteen-day battle with myxomatosis.[11] His sisters were present at his death, and more than 10,000 rabbits attended his funeral.[12] Memorials were held as far away as Japan. Peter Rabbit is buried in his home garden, and his gravesite is visited by thousands of rabbits each year.

Recent Developments

In 1956, a descendant of Flopsy Bunny, Mrs. Ami Bunny, found a collection of drawings by Peter in a tin beneath the floorboards of the cottage where Peter and his sisters spent their childhood. Ami was conducting a restoration of the cottage for its 1960 declaration as a World Historical Site. She donated the tin and its contents to The Peter Rabbit Society, which raises funds for *Planned Rabbithood*.[13]

The drawings are on permanent display at the Peter Rabbit Museum. Art Historian Mona Twitterwill published an academic study on the pieces, entitled "Methodologies of Speaking Secret Histories: The Hidden Art of Peter Rabbit." In her study, Twitterwill posits that Peter Rabbit's troubled childhood was a direct result of the incidents that occurred in Mr. McGregor's garden on the occasion that led to his father's disappearance.[14]

For years the public, and Peter's family, assumed that Peter's father had been baked into a pie by Mrs. McGregor. But Twitterwill has a new interpretation based on Peter's drawings. "Many of these pieces are sketches of young rabbits that have eerie similarities to Peter's own siblings. You might argue that these similarities are due to Peter using his sisters as models; however, there are pronounced discrepancies in fur coloring between photographs of Flopsy, Mopsy, and Cotton-tail and the found sketches."[15] Twitterwill theorizes that the sketches show the faces of Peter's half-siblings.

Investigations of the abandoned McGregor homestead have found cages in the backyard and a framed article from a local human paper showing the farmer McGregor holding two dead rabbits by their ears. A blue ribbon is pinned to McGregor's jacket.[16]

Incidents of rabbit disappearances in the Meadow area due to trappings sharply declined in the period after Mr. Rabbit's disappearance, according to a 1905 study conducted by Field University.[17] It is believed by some that Mr. Rabbit was used as a breeding hare due to his lustrous pelt. [Verification Needed]

"Viewing a loved one as dead is easier for families to cope with," says psychologist Irene Badger. "It is likely that Peter chose to tell his mother that his father was dead in order for her to have closure. However, for Peter, knowing that his father was alive was a constant torment for him. And this, not his love for cabbage and carrots, is what drove him again and again to return to the McGregor's garden."[18]

The Friends of the Peter Rabbit Society plan to hold fundraisers, including a Chamomile Tea Festival, to raise money for a memorial statue of Peter with his father.[19]

Notes/References

1   "Peter Rabbit's Rough Youth: Sisters Tell All." *The Weekly Carrot.* 18 March 1907.

2   Oshima, Amami. "Special Report: An Intimate Interview with Peter Rabbit's Mother." RBBT 42 News. 1907. Archived at headquarters of the Peter Rabbit Society.

3   "Promo for Peter Rabbit Special – Old, 1907." YouTube. Retrieved 27 June 2012.

4   Glire, Mo. "His Journey Was My Own: A Book Review of *The Tale of Peter Rabbit.*" *The Lagomorph Times.* 13 June 1907.

5   "New Poll Shows that 83% of New Mothers Read *The Tale of Peter Rabbit* Aloud Every Night." *Burrow Guardian.* 20 August 1907.

6   "Kits in a Thief's Arms: A Photographic Survey of Newspaper Appearances by Peter Rabbit, 1907-1909." *The Journal of Lagomorph Psychology,* 30.4 (1989): 61- 72. Print.

7   "Photograph: Peter Rabbit's Arrest." *The Meadow Gazette.* 25 July 1910. Retrieved 17 June 2011.

8   "Sales of *The Tale of Peter Rabbit* Tumble." *The Burrow Times Review of Books.* 6 August 1910.

9   "Photograph Archive: The Unpublished Publicity Photographs of Peter Rabbit." *Burrow Guardian.*12 March 2009.

10 "Where is He Now? Peter Rabbit Edition." YouTube. Original airdate: 2008. MTV. Retrieved 25 May 2012.

11 County of Meadows Department of Health Services. (2012). Peter Rabbit death certificate.

12 "Tens of Thousands Migrate to the Meadows to Mourn Peter Rabbit." *The Meadow Gazette.* 23 February 1912.

13 "New Donations Report: 1956." *Does and Kits: The Monthly Newsletter of Planned Rabbithood.* September 1956.

14 Twitterwill, Mona. "Methodologies of Speaking Secret Histories: The Hidden Art of Peter Rabbit." *Lost Voices: A Journal of Newly Found Celebrity Art.* 3.7 (2007): 35–42. Print.

15 Ibid. p. 42.

16 "Breeding to Win: A Journey into Farmer McGregor's Garden." *The Lagomorph Times.* 4 April 2008.

17 National Association of Pelt Suppliers. *Trappings Record: 1900 – 1905.* Field University Press. 1906.

18 Badger, Irene. "Trapped in the Garden Forever: An Analysis of the Drawings of a Young Peter Rabbit." *The Journal of Lagomorph Psychology* 17.4 (2008): 15 – 26. Print.

19 "Upcoming Events: First Annual Chamomile Tea Festival Fundraiser." *Does and Kits: The Monthly Newsletter of Planned Rabbithood.* October 2011.

Secrets of Flatland

Anne Toole

Secrets of Flatland

The underground publication of Flatland, A Romance of Many Dimensions,[1] served as wake-up call for many Figures in Flatland that all was not as it seemed. The author, a Square, shared his perspective of the history of Flatland and unfortunately carried many of the false assumptions perpetrated by Flatland's leadership. Although hinted at in the text, Flatland is not a world of perfect balance, but one of intrigue, oppression, and hope.

Societal Secrets

The greatest secret of Flatland is that anyone can achieve a high degree of intelligence, if properly trained from an early age. In order to hide this fact, the Circles created a system wherein women and the lower classes have no access to education, and those that show a predisposition toward learning on their own are quickly bred to produce Figures of a higher class. Common cultural beliefs do the rest.

Nowhere is this secret more dangerous than in the case of women. Unlike men, they can easily move among the classes without regard to birth or appearance. The laws of Flatland are thus most strict with regard to women. Masquerading as safety measures, the laws serve to distract society from the fact that women are not offered education on par with the men of their class.

Secret Societies

Circle Assassins

Women's versatility and ability to become essentially invisible proved to be too big an asset to ignore. The Circles trained a cadre of women who would act as spies and assassins in the lower rungs of society. Women already showed a natural talent to imitate the lower classes and easily infiltrated seditious groups at all levels of society. Women reported back on activities and acted quickly to suppress dangerous ideas, usually with extreme prejudice. As these instances became more frequent, the Circles took steps to bury the truth with misleading news reports.

In one well-publicized case, a woman killed her husband and children, cleaned up the mess, then asked where her husband and children had gone.[2] The official version reinforced the belief in women's low intelligence, tendency to act irrationally, and inability to remember crucial information. In fact, the husband in question was a Square Society member who had been running an underground news organization. The assassin had killed and replaced his real wife. Upon discovering that the Square was passing down seditious tendencies to the second generation and as a warning to other Society members, she made the decision to take the entire family out.

The Square Society

The Square Society grew out of the Chromatic Sedition and was founded by a Square survivor of the Universal Colour Bill Massacre. [3] Although named after the founder, the Square Society boasts members from all ranks of society, including, it is said, some members of the Circular class. The Society aims to bring greater equality to Flatland.

The Circles have long maintained a policy of euthanasia to end deformity, and the Square Society found natural allies in the parents of deformed children. The Society found a great ally in one such woman, a Circle wife who had an unlikely affair with an Isosceles Triangle. When she bore an Irregular Triangle, she fretted not only for her child's life, but for her own. The Society stepped in, offering a trade. They would hide her son and give her a girl whose mother had been killed in the line of duty. In return, she would owe the Society a favor. She currently supplies information about the Circles, and the Society is trying to get information about the Circle leader.

The Square Society smuggles condemned children away by surrounding them with Triangles pretending to be Irregular. They secrete them in the lowest ranks of society, often in the homes of sympathetic Soldiers and Workers. The Society has been raising these outcasts as a new rank of teachers, who go into the Working Class and educate children in secret.

In recent years, the Circles have taken more extreme measures to suppress the Society. At a general meeting that consisted of half the leadership, one of the women proved to be a Circle assassin and destroyed everyone present. One Square escaped, as did one woman, who carefully hid in plain sight. With some controversy, the Square Society quickly adopted many of the techniques of the Circles. Upon realizing the importance of women in the Circles' subjugation of the lower classes, they have themselves placed women in the higher echelons as double agents. Currently, the Square Society counts as one of its heads a Woman from the Hexagon class, who has infiltrated higher Polygon society.

The Rise of Sepheron

The Circles have had complete control of Flatland for generations. In recent years, their measures of repression have become even more draconian; more and more they resort to institutionalizing or destroying anyone who disagrees with their policies. The Circles themselves have begun to feel the pinch, as the current leader, Sepheron, has grown secretive. Few claim to have met this leader in person, and of those who claim it, none can offer proof. Sepheron shows an uncanny ability to be aware of what is going on, and Circle Society is rife with distrust and censorship. Some suspect a spy is among them; others believe Sepheron to be some sort of devil. The Circles find relief in the fact that Sepheron has no wife and thus has produced no heir, and all hope his policies will die with him. They are wrong on all counts.

Sepheron is in fact a Sphere from Spaceland. A renegade in his own country for his beliefs in a Fourth Dimension, he happened upon the existence of Flatland a generation ago. Preferring to be perceived as a god in one country, rather than a lunatic in another, Sepheron took the place of an Irregular Circle that had been sentenced to die. He has been living as a two-dimensional circle for years. However, as a Sphere, he can see quite a distance in either direction, and keep tabs on those closest to him. When the Gospel of the Three Dimensions found its way to Flatland, Sepheron had to clamp down on the supposed heresy in order to keep his secret. Because he has no ability to reproduce in the two-dimensional realm, he has ordered experiments on the Irregulars banished to the sanitarium to see if he might still produce offspring. However, as a Solid, he can live over a thousand years, so he is in no hurry.

Notes/References

1   A Square (2007). *Flatland: A Romance of Many Dimensions*. Abbot Edition (unabridged). Devonford.

2   Quadratur, Lieam (1998). "Family slain by wife and mother." *The Sunday Line*. Devonford. Retrieved 2007-12-3.

3   Orbus, J. ed. (1990). *Chromatistes, a History*. Circle Publications. Heloq. Discusses the man who painted the

Figures, fomented a revolution, and forced the Circles to end Figure confusion with a bloody massacre.

See Also

- Flatland
- Chromatistes
- Geometry

Sanyo TM-300 Home-Use Time Machine

Jeremy Sim

Sanyo TM-300 Home-Use Time Machine

* It is proposed that this article be deleted because of the following concerns:

- no evidence of reliable sources.

- who wrote this?

The **Sanyo TM-300** (introduced August 2009) is the third generation of <u>home-use time machines</u> from <u>SANYO Electric Co.</u> The TM line is marketed primarily towards <u>DIY</u> enthusiasts and culinary professionals, and features major improvements over the preceding <u>TM-200</u> design. The TM-300 is equipped with <u>face recognition</u> technology, and has the ability to "undo" up to 30 seconds, exceeding the previous upper limit of 16.67 seconds.

Like its predecessors, the TM-300 works by creating a small "pocket" of <u>recessed time</u> (around 2 cubic meters) in which the user can safely redo an action or a sequence of actions. The user experiences the time interval twice, while an individual outside the time pocket only observes the most recent redo.

TM-300 refers to the development codename and model name used by Sanyo in its Asia and Oceania distribution regions. In North America and Europe, the TM-300 is marketed under the name Sanyo W3lls, a stylized reference to author <u>H.G. Wells</u>.

As of March 31, 2010, Sanyo TM time machines have sold over 158.75 million units worldwide, making them the best-selling time machine product to date.

CONTENTS

Hardware

The TM-300 is housed in a silver-white chassis, and retains the indented spherical shape of its predecessors. Prior to release, the matte white surface led many to refer to the TM-300 as Project Pearl.[citation needed]

The upper surface of the TM-300 is overlaid with a touchscreen, designed to accept input from a user's gloved or ungloved fingers. The TM-300 also features a front-facing camera and microphone and supports wireless standards.

The system boots using Sanyo's proprietary firmware. A health and safety warning is displayed first, followed by the main menu. In addition to accepting voice and face commands, the overhauled main menu presents users with four options: Undo, Set an Auto-Undo Trigger, Manage Profiles, and Adjust Settings.

Technology and Features

Probably a bad idea to leave this one out there.

Health Effects

Irrelevant.

Development History

Not sure anymore.

- edited by amorris, 08:41 5 September 2010

Listen up, people. I'm hijacking this page with an important message.

At six-something this morning, a YouTube user named sanjay31 posted a video tutorial showing people how to daisy-chain TM-300 units together using a simple hack. It's now 8:17 am, less than two hours later, and the video is gone. Not just the YouTube video itself, but sanjay31's channel too, and all the archived copies of

ANY of sanjay's videos ANYWHERE on the internet. I found some other videos and eHows trying to explain the same thing, but sanjay31's is gone. It's like sanjay31 never existed.

Something's happening, and I'm not sure I want to know what.

The tutorial showed how to extend the ten-second Undo limitation to a potentially unlimited amount of time, provided one had enough TM-300s lying around. It was a brilliant hack, sanjay. But you should never have posted that video. If you'd read my blog post on the limitations of TM-300 firmware, you'd see why. I think it's theoretically possible for someone with a pair of rooted TM-300s to use your daisy-chain method and manipulate a pocket of time much larger than currently possible. By my calculation, such a pocket would be quite a bit larger than the Earth.

Yeah. If I'm right, that means the scum of the internet just got the ability to edit reality.

I don't know if I'm being paranoid. Maybe sanjay31 realized the danger, and deleted his Youtube account himself. But I have a strong feeling that things are changing, and not in a good way.

I feel at least a little responsible for this, so I'm vandalizing this Wiki page to send a message to any noobs out there who are thinking of using these hacks for evil:

DON'T EVEN THINK ABOUT IT PEOPLE. THIS IS NOT A JOKE. THIS IS NOT WIKIPEDIA, WHERE YOU CAN EDIT THE COLLECTED KNOWLEDGE OF MANKIND FOR A QUICK LOL. THIS IS REAL LIFE.

I advise anyone who owns a TM-300 to destroy it now, or bring it to a safe location among trusted friends. If I'm right, there will be idiots going back in time to kill Hitler. There will be jackasses lining up at JFK. As sure as God made little green apples, there will be vandals. Please, please, please let there be counter-vandals too. I will be one of them, if it comes to it. We can fix everything they break. We can preserve it. And if the only way is to go back and edit out the existence of time machines, so be it.

My name is Ann Morrison, and it is September 5th, 2010. This will be a mess bigger than anything we have ever seen, but when the dust settles and our shared reality is determined for good by the most vicious and persistent, I hope at least this Wikipedia entry is still here.

- edited by amorris, 09:59 5 September 2010
- edited by amorris, 10:03 5 September 2010

See Also

- Comparison of home-use time machines
- Sanyo time machines
- Time machine

Elizabeth Burgoyne Corbett

L. Timmel Duchamp

Elizabeth Burgoyne Corbett

Elizabeth Burgoyne Corbett (2346-2431), a citizen of New Amazonia, was born in Andersonia to John Burgoyne, a carpenter, and Maria Corbett, a scientist attached to the <u>Central Dietetic Hospital of Andersonia</u>. Corbett held the <u>Eve Fawcett Chair in Ethical Studies</u> at <u>New Cambridge College</u> and served a term in the Government as a Privy Councilor. She is best known, however, as the author of the pioneering *New Amazonia: a foretaste of the future*, which has been widely hailed as the first known example of the literary form known as "<u>the alien visitation fable</u>," which is always set in the future and typically features visitors from elsewhere (in the case of *New Amazonia*, the distant past), satirizing or in other ways estranging practices and ideas the author wishes to question. It was in her *New Amazonia* that the expression "feminine nincompoopity" first appeared (launching its apparently permanent presence in colloquial <u>speech</u>, along with the numerous other forms it spawned, viz. "masculine nincompoopity," "childish nincompoopity," "pedagogical nincompoopity," "political nincompoopity," "benign nincompoopity," "naïve nincompoopity," etc.).

CONTENTS

Life

Until the age of ten, when she entered the educational system, Corbett divided her time between the usual informal childhood pursuits, her father's workshop (where she learned the basic skills of carpentering and constructed objects ranging from toys to artifacts to small practical items), and reading, which she taught herself to do at the age of three. At age ten she entered Andersonia's <u>Honor School</u>, which she left early, after four years, to enter <u>Besant College</u>. She was awarded a Bachelor's degree, with Full Honors, in 2363, and was valedictorian of her class. She then attended <u>Forbes College</u>, where she studied <u>philosophy</u> and the <u>dietetic sciences</u>, in which she received corresponding doctorates in 2366 and 2368.

Corbett worked for twelve years as a <u>laboratory</u> director at the <u>North-Central Dietetic Hospital</u> in <u>Stanton Heights</u> in <u>North-Central New Amazonia</u>. She published more than two dozen research papers during this time, and made a stir with her paper "Some ethical considerations concerning <u>mental health</u> issues," which she published in 2382 in *Ethics and the Soul*. Scholars have identified 2382 as a seminal year in Corbett's philosophical development.[1] In 2385, she became a Deputy Adviser for Medical Affairs in the <u>county government</u> of North-Central New Amazonia. She continued publishing papers exploring ethical questions about proposed changes in Government policies for the mentally ill.

In 2390, <u>New Cambridge College</u> offered her the <u>Eve Fawcett Chair in Ethical Studies</u>, which she held until her death. While she held this prestigious post, she served on a variety of Government committees and from 2401-2406 as a <u>Privy Councilor</u>. Her term as a Privy Councilor was stormy.[2]

She published her first <u>novel</u>, *New Amazonia: a foretaste of the future,* in 2407, in which she satirized the permanent platform of the <u>Standards & Values Party</u> (S&VP) in general and policy proposals that Leader Cowley's <u>Prime Advisers</u> were urging the Privy Councilors to enact, and in at least one case, one of the Prime Advisers, in particular.[3] The novel was set in a future—2472—in which the S&VP's mandates had been fully enacted, but made the point, by casting a woman from Victorian <u>England</u> as its main character that the social, economic, and political results of imposing the S&VP's dearest wishes on New Amazonia, that these were such as would greatly appeal to a morally archaic English person. Corbett made her satiric intent explicit, even going so far as to lift an entire <u>sentence</u> out of the S&VP's Permanent Platform and put it into the <u>mouth</u> of a woman meant to represent "ordinary" people, one "Mrs. Saville":

> To encourage anything that produces physical deterioration is to retard our chances of attaining spiritual perfection and is too dear a price to pay for such unsatisfactory results.

The novel created an uproar, not only in the political sphere, but also in literary circles. Most critics lambasted it for being scientifically and technologically "muddled" (a muddle a few critics praised as being appropriate, given that the first-person narrator was supposed to have a crude, pre-modern understanding of <u>science</u>), but since the book enjoyed ten printings in its first year alone, numerous novelists produced their own "alien visitation fables" (as the form soon came to be known), and led to the <u>fashion</u> of depicting future consequences of policies under consideration, most satirical, but a growing number exhorting the benefits of this or that proposed reform or abolition.

Corbett published her only book-length work of ethics in 2412. [4] Although this was well-received, its audience was small, especially in comparison with *New Amazonia*. Perhaps for that reason, her remaining books were all novels (though she continued to publish papers concerned with the ethical and practical effects of mental health policies). Her greatest achievement is generally agreed to be the crafting and passage of the <u>Mental Health Reform Act of 2428</u>.[5]

Corbett died in a boating <u>accident</u> in 2431. Her unpublished work and private papers are archived at New Cambridge College and will become available for public examination and scholarly citation in 2531.

Works

Corbett's philosophical and literary works all strove to achieve a thorough-going reformulation of ethical and moral thought. Her magnum opus, *Book of Ethics,* insisted that for <u>utilitarianism</u> to truly serve the <u>commonweal</u>, the advanced technological has an obligation to include all its members, including those who are relegated to the margins of "the strong, healthy citizenry." Though an argument might be made for the validity of pre-modern societies excluding the weak and nonproductive from society's protection and nurturance, the conditions allowing such a rationalization no longer existed. The fact that New Amazonia, rather than broadening its definition of the commonweal, was actually considering further narrowing it, was according to Corbett, morally indefensible.

Corbett's first novel, *New Amazonia,* offered a satirical treatment of the S&VP's proposal to euthanize those deemed incurably insane and terminate all fetuses with <u>genetic abnormalities</u>. Several critics have noted that the novel inextricably linked the <u>Religion of the Mother</u> (which the S&VP argues ought to be made the official state religion of New Amazonia) with the use of <u>euthanasia</u> and <u>abortion</u> to cull the weak and <u>disabled</u>.[6] Other opponents of the S&VP adopted that linkage, which soon became established in the public mind. <u>Verena Lester</u> bitterly observed in a speech in 2413 that "Thanks to Lizzie Corbett, as far as the public is concerned, the Religion of the Mother is all about enforcing cruel policies against the helpless and defenseless."[7]

Corbett published a sequel to *New Amazonia* in 2419, *The Mother's Will.* In this sequel, *New Amazonia's* secondary buffoonish character Augustus Fitz-Musicus returns to the future New Amazonia not in 2472, but in 2501, with a woman based on someone who actually existed, <u>Emma Goldman</u>, a Russian anarchist. Although *New Amazonia* has many humorous, even comical moments in it, *The Mother's Will* is riotously funny—and notoriously bawdy. The S&VP was so outraged by this novel they tried to bring suit against the government's <u>Department of the Censor</u>.[citation needed] *The Mother's Will* went through eighteen printings in its first year. It has been dramatized for the stage four times and has been the basis for several films. It also inspired new interest in nineteenth- and twentieth-century European <u>history</u> and the Irish and French wars with England.

Three of Corbett's novels—*A Grand Day, What They Did Next, and Will o' the Wisp*—are fantastical comedies of manners with relatively gentle explorations of the grim themes of mental health, disability, and <u>old age</u>. Each went out of print after their fourth printings. *Alice O'Reilly's Aunt*, which has a lateral <u>association </u>with *New Amazonia* (one of the minor characters in that novel was a domestic worker, Alice O'Reilly), is Corbett's most conventional novel. It has probably stayed in print simply because of its tenuous association with *New Amazonia*.[citation needed]

The Alien Visitation Fable

As far as literary scholars are concerned, Corbett's forging of the "alien visitation fable" is her greatest claim to fame.[8] Apart from spawning innumerable imitations, it also set the stage for the development of the "future consequences" genre, which dispenses with alien visitors altogether and simply sets the narrative in the near (or even distant) future.[9] The means by which an alien visitor is transported to New Amazonia's future became an increasingly important variable in the alien visitation fable. Corbett's original means was the hallucination/drug fantasy. Others followed this lead by using medical <u>coma</u>, ordinary <u>dreams</u>, <u>nightmare</u>, and <u>daydreams</u>, each of which set a particular tone through which to read the author's depiction of a future reality. But these methods eventually began to pall on readers. Corbett's sequel to *New Amazonia, The Mother's Will,* introduced a German <u>teleportation device</u>—proposing that the <u>quantum particle</u> experiments of twentieth-century German scientists had actually succeeded in moving living animals (and not just coded information) between two distant points in space (and time). Other writers quickly adopted this means, until it became nearly the de rigueur method for the genre. This changed only when <u>Colleen Collins</u>, in 2439, made her alien visitors star-travelers from across the galaxy. Visits from Galactic travelers (often en masse), too, became wildly popular and led to the depiction of vast geopolitical conspiracies (usually focused on the struggle between <u>Germany</u> and <u>Russia</u> or <u>Japan</u> and <u>Indochina</u>, or <u>Indochina</u> and <u>China</u>). Collins wrote a series of these, in one of which the alien visitor attempted to assist very near-future Germany in a <u>campaign</u> of <u>subversion</u> of New Amazonia through the covert distribution of <u>personal computers</u> to children as <u>toys</u>.

Excerpts from *New Amazonia*

One of the most effective — and certainly the most famous — passage in *New Amazonia* is the conversation, near the end of the book, in which the character of Principal Grey (which many critics have identified as a caricature of <u>Sarah Palin Montague</u>, founder of the S&VP) advises her visiting Victorian interlocutor that her traveling companion will probably have to be euthanized, given his apparent incurable insanity:

> "I am afraid," was the rejoinder, "that Mr. Fitz-Musicus can never be converted into a sober New Amazonian. He has revolted against wearing our National costume and says that rather than sacrifice his British individuality, and look like everybody else, he will brave the probability of becoming a laughing-stock, and that he will wear his old clothes to rags rather than have his individuality swallowed up in a general resemblance to every nincompoop in the country. I am afraid it would necessitate him to live as long again as he has done, to bring him into the exact likeness of a native of New Amazonia. But his vanity is inextinguishable, and nothing could bring him to the belief that his appearance does not eclipse that of our

handsomest men. When last I heard of him, he was seeking some stuff with a large pattern. He says that if he can find a nice big check, he may perhaps consent to have a suit made in native style, but he is not at all sure yet."

"But how does he intend earning his living?"

"He is not at all sure about that either. He says he will think about it. But he protests meanwhile very bitterly against a destiny that has placed him among people who can be sordid and vulgar enough to ask him, the pampered scion of a great house, to degrade himself by attempting to earn his own living. He considers that the Mother ought to be proud of being honoured by his sojourn amongst us, and that she ought to be only too glad to extend her hospitality indefinitely to him.

"And the Mother—what does she think of his peculiarities? Are they found annoying?"

"Well, to a certain extent, yes. We abhor ingratitude. But in this case, we are being forced into the belief that this Englishman is not exactly a responsible agent. I am afraid that he is not quite sane. But, of course, unless he becomes very much worse, it will not be found necessary to adopt stringent measures with him."

"And if his peculiarities should become much more pronounced?

"Ah, then—then, we shall be compelled to do something. He has already lost so much time during his prolonged state of unconsciousness, that it will be a charity to release his spirit, if it becomes evident that it is withheld from further progress towards Heavenly bliss by being confined in a body which is more likely to promote retrogression than progression."

As I listened to this calm utterance my blood positively ran cold. Full well I knew what she meant. The peculiar

tenets of New Amazonian religion had been carefully explained to me, and I knew that the life of Mr. Fitz-Musicus
was destined to be a short one, unless he restored the native belief in his sanity. I was quite unable to talk much
more after this, and my friend, observing that I seemed
fatigued and had better rest, left me to my own resourc-
es. But I felt incapable of resting, for I was too excited.
Clearly the life of the eccentric Augustus was in danger,
and I was impatient to see him and warn him without
delay.

Another passage, near the beginning, when the visitors are getting their first look at New Amazonia, is popular for its hilarity:

The next event I can chronicle was opening my eyes on
a scene at once so beautiful and strange that I started
to my feet in amaze. This was not my study, and I beheld nothing of the magazine, which was the last thing
I remembered seeing before I went to sleep. I was in a
glorious garden, gay with brilliant hued flowers, the fra-
grance of which filled the air with a subtle and delicate
perfume; around me were trees laden with luscious fruits,
which I can only compare to apples, pears, and quinces,
only they were as much finer than the fruits I had hitherto
been familiar with as Ribstone pippins are to crabs, and as
jargonelles are to greenjacks. Countless birds were singing
overhead, and I was about to sink down again and yield
to a delicious languor which overpowered me, when I was
recalled to the necessity of behaving more decorously by
hearing someone near me exclaim in mystified accents,
"By Jove! But isn't this extraordinary? I say, do you live
here, or have you been taking hasheesh too?"

I looked up, and saw, perched on the limb of a great tree,
a young man of about thirty years of age, who looked so
ridiculously mystified at the elevated position in which
he found himself that I could not refrain from smiling,

though I did not feel able to give an immediate satisfactory reply to his queries.

"Oh, that's right," he commented. "It makes a fellow relieved to see a smile, when he wasn't at all sure whether he wouldn't get sent to Jericho for perching up an apple tree. But really, I don't know how the deuce I came to be up here, that is, I beg your pardon, but I can't understand how I happen to be up this apple tree. And oh! by Jove! it isn't an apple tree, after all! Isn't it extraordinary?"

But I could positively do nothing but laugh at him for the space of a moment or two. Then I gravely remarked that as I supposed he was not glued to the tree, he had better come down, whereat he followed my advice, being unfortunate enough, however, to graze his hands, and tear the knees of his trousers during the process of disembarkation.

When at last he had relieved himself of a few spare expletives, delivered in a tone which he vainly flattered himself was too low for me to hear, he stood revealed before me, a perfect specimen of the British masher. His height was not too great, being, I subsequently ascertained, five feet three, an inch less than my own, but he made the most of what there was of him by holding himself as erect as possible, and as he wore soles an inch thick to his otherwise smart boots, he looked rather taller than he really was.

His proportions were not at all bad, and I have seen a good many very much worse looking fellows who flattered themselves that they were quite killing. His face had lost the freshness of early youth, and looked as though it spent a great deal of its time in the haunts of dissipation. The moustache, however, was perfect—so golden, so long, so elegant was it, that it must have been the envy of countless members of the masher tribe, and I was not surprised to notice presently that its owner found his pet occupation in stroking it.

Just now, however, he was chiefly employed in lamenting the accident which had occurred to his nether garment, this being, by the way, one portion of a tweed suit of the most alarming demonstrative pattern and colour.

"By Jove!" he muttered, disconsolately, "it's awful! you know. When I was so careful, too! What on earth ever possessed me to mount that tree? Isn't it extraordinary?"

This time I was just about to attempt a reply, when I was struck dumb with awe and astonishment, and my companion, who had found his own eyes sufficiently powerful to take in my appearance, hastily fixed a single eyeglass into position, and gazed in open-mouthed wonder at an apparition which approached us.

And he might well gaze, for of a surety the creature which we saw was something worth looking at, and a specimen of a race the like of which we had never seen before. "It is a woman," I thought. "A goddess!" the masher declared, and for a time I could not feel sure that he was mistaken.

She was close upon seven feet in height, I am sure, and was of magnificent build. A magnified Venus, a glorified Hebe, a smiling Juno were here all united in one perfect human being, whose gait was the very poetry of motion.

She wore a very peculiar dress, I thought, until I saw that science and common sense had united in forming a costume in which the requirements alike of health, comfort, and beauty had reached their acme.

A modification of the divided skirt came a little below the knee, the stockings and laced boots serving to heighten, instead of to hide, their owner's beautiful symmetry of limb. A short skirt supplemented the graceful tunic, which was worn slightly open at the neck, and partially revealed the dainty whiteness of a shapely bust. The costume was of black velvet, set off by exquisite filmy laces and a crimson sash that confined the tunic at the waist and hung gracefully on the left side of the wearer.

She was wearing a silver-embroidered velvet cap, which she courteously doffed on beholding us, and I noticed that her hair, but an inch or two long, curled about her head and temples in the most delightfully picturesque fashion imaginable.

She was surprised to see us, that was quite apparent, but she evidently mistook our identity for a while. "What strange children!" she exclaimed, in a rich, sonorous voice, which was bewitchingly musical. "Why are you here, and for what particular purpose are you masquerading in this extraordinary fashion?"

"Yes, it is extraordinary, isn't it?" burst forth the masher," but you are slightly mistaken about us. I can't answer for this lady, and I really don't know what the deuce she is doing here, but I am the Honourable Augustus Fitz-Musicus. I daresay you have heard of me. My ancestor, you know, was King George the Fourth. He fell in love with a very beautiful lady, who, until the first gentleman in Europe favoured her with his attentions, was an opera singer. She subsequently became the mother of a family, who were all provided for by their delighted father, the king. The eldest son was created Duke of Fitz-Musicus, and he and his family were endowed with a perpetual pension for 'distinguished services rendered to the State,' you know."

"Then you are not a little boy?" queried the giantess. "But of course you must be. Come here, my little dear, and tell me who taught you to say those funny things, and who pasted that queer little moustache on your face."

As she spoke she actually stooped, kissed the Honourable Augustus Fitz-Musicus on the forehead, and patted him playfully on the cheek with one shapely finger. This was, however, an indignity not to be borne patiently, and the recipient of these well-meant attentions indignantly sprang on one side, his face scarlet, and his voice tremulous with humiliated wrath.

"How dare you?" he gasped. "How dare you insult me so? You must know that I am not a child. Your own hugeness need not prevent you from seeing that _I am a man._"

"A man! Never! O, this is too splendid a joke to enjoy by myself." Saying this, and laughing until the tears came into her eyes, the goddess raised her voice a little, and called to some companions who were evidently close at hand, "Myra! Hilda! Agnes! Oh, do come quickly. I have found two such curious creatures."

In response to this summons three more girls of gigantic stature came from the further end of the garden, and completed our discomfiture by joining in the laugh against us.

"What funny little things! Wherever did you find them, Dora?" queried one of the newcomers, whereat Dora composed her risible faculties as well as she was able, and explained that she had just found us where we were, and that one of us claimed to be a _man._

Myra and Agnes were quite as amused at this as Dora had been, but Hilda took the situation somewhat more seriously. She had noted how furious the Honourable Augustus Fitz-Musicus looked, and observed my vain attempt to assume a dignified demeanour in the presence of such a formidable array of playful goddesses, who now all plied us with questions together.

I did not feel much inclined to converse, for I was terribly afraid of being ridiculed. But Hilda questioned me so much more sensibly, in my opinion, than the others, that I was disposed to be more communicative to her than to them.

"Where do you come from?" she questioned gently, as if she were afraid of injuring me by using her normal voice.

"I am English," I replied proudly, feeling quite sure that the very name of my beloved native land would prove a talisman of value in any part of the globe. But although the beautiful quartette refrained from laughing, they listened to me in mystified astonishment, partly, I perceived, because my small voice was a revelation to them, and partly because my answer conveyed no understandable meaning to them.

"English," at last said Agnes. "What do you mean by English? There is no such nation now. I believe that centuries ago Teutoscotland used to be called England, and that used to be inhabited by the English, a warlike race which is now extinct."

"My dear Agnes," interposed Hilda, "You surely forget that we are ourselves descended from this great race. But suppose we go on with our questions. Not so fast, my little man; here, I will take care of you for the present."

The last exclamation was evoked by an attempt on the part of the Honourable Augustus to escape while the attention of the party was concentrated upon myself. He was, however, foiled in his attempt, and Hilda coolly seated him upon a tall garden seat, as if he were a baby, and kept a detaining hand on his wrist, while she listened to the replied I now made to my tormentors. "What is your name?" was the next interrogatory to which I was subjected. I did not consider it necessary to go into details, so merely gave my name. Other questions were now asked me, but I was so determined to give no food for ridicule, if I could help it, that I was rather obstinate in refusing information, and at last took refuge in the remark, delivered as quietly as my tingling nerves would permit, "That in my country people were polite to strangers, and did not interrogate them as if they were so many wild beasts."

Even while giving utterance to this remark, I remembered several scenes which proved that it was far from true. But the goddesses did not know this much, and my reproof served to convince them that the Honourable Augustus and myself were not monkeys that had learnt the art of speech and been dressed for exhibition, but actual, though very queer, specimens of the human race divine.

Apologies for their rudeness were now freely tendered by the giantesses, and one of them proposed to take us into the house at once and supply us with refreshments. No sooner said than done, and I hardly know whether I was most amused or humiliated to find myself led by the hand, as if I were only just learning to walk and must be carefully guarded from stumbling.

It was some consolation to observe that the Honourable Augustus was served likewise and that he was lifted up the huge steps, which must be ascended to enter the house, just as easily as I was. We were taken into a large hall, which seemingly served as a refectory, for I observed a table in the centre, upon which many covers were laid.

Mental Health Reform Act

The pinnacle of Corbett's achievement was unquestionably the passage of the Mental Health Reform Act of 2428, which she had been working toward all her adult life. It is disputable whether her fiction, particularly her first novel, had the most to do with generating the sea change in public thought, or her years of work in philosophy and the dietetic sciences. Some have argued that the S&VP pushed the notion of the only true citizen being a healthy adult to its breaking point, and that no sane person would have endorsed the "policy reforms" (as Sarah Palin Montague termed her purportedly religious campaign for the elimination of the incurably diseased) and that therefore the Mental Health Reform Act of 2428 was only legislating the existing commonsense understanding of ethics.[10]

Legacy

Corbett's legacy was two-fold. Her contributions to popular literature, while not great works in themselves, gave birth to a new field of popular literature, one that has encouraged the engagement of fiction with social and political issues. Many literary critics deplore this development, but scholars of literary history agree that this is a significant development that has gradually begun to impact every area of literary production. Her contributions to ethics and state policy cannot be overstated. A historian of philosophy, writing an appreciation of Corbett on the occasion of Corbett's death, hailed her as "the most significant New Amazonian philosopher in two centuries."[11]

Notes/References

1   Inter alia, Margaret Arnold Fortescue, "The Origins of Elizabeth Burgoyne Corbett's Ethical Questioning," *History and Philosophy*, 122, 4 (2450); Jerome Anson Burroughs, *Elizabeth Burgoyne Corbett: The Life*, New Andersonia, 2458, pp. 79-86.

2   See Burroughs, pp. 337-380, and Leah Johnson Velazquez, *Chronicle of a Government Divided within Itself: the Cowley Administration, 2399-2409*, New Andersonia, 2440, pp. 1-4; 24-31; 108-137; and passim.

3   See Burroughs, pp. 337-425, Charlotte Baker Bolton, "Reading *New Amazonia* as Satire," Annals of Literature 245, 6 (2412), and Arlene Stanton Thewes, *The Alien Visitation Fable: An Analytical History*, New Andersonia, 2451.

4   *Quality of Life in a Decent World: Considerations of Values and Standards*, New Andersonia, 2412.

5   See particularly Jerome Anson Burroughs, *Elizabeth Burgoyne Corbett: The Life*, New Andersonia, 2458.

6   See especially Bolton and Burroughs.

7   Verena Lester, "Cruel Calumnies," in *Proceedings of the Annual Convention of the Standards and Values Party*, 33, New Andersonia, 2413.

8   *New Directions in New Amazonian Literature*, ed. Eileen Gunn Gonzalez, New Weldon, 2476.

9   Sharon Lee Fulmer, "Future Consequences Fiction: Its brief and often vexed history," *Annals of Literature* 256, 3 (2433). See also Thewes, pp. 231-45.

10 Martha Luisa Donnelly, "An Expected Victory for Commonsense," *The Capital Daily News*, 9 June 2428.

11 John Mathers Yeats, "Elizabeth Burgoyne Corbett (2346-2431): A Life Well Spent," *North-Central Times*, 14 March 2431.

God

Anna Tambour

God

~#+* Joe Al "*!*!*" ("The Father") God (October 3, -45BKE --) is an international celebrity/dictator/terrorist/purported inventor/ protection magnate/writer.

[NOTE: This entry lacks appropriate documentation for many of its assertions. Citations desperately needed.]

CONTENTS

Biography

Early Life

Born to a middle-class suburban-nomad family on the South Side of as-yet (2012) undiscovered <u>dwarf sub-planet 8943-P789</u>, the exact date of God's birth cannot be confirmed, because parish records were destroyed by fire in 1968 and before that, there was no Wikipedia.

What is surmised, however, with only lukewarm debate, is that from early life, God had problems. His mother is thought to have suffered from <u>dermatosis</u>, the side-effect of which was that she did not carry God with her when she gleaned, neither in her mouth, nor on her back, nor in a pram or fold-up walker. The family would not have been of the class to engage a nursemaid, though studies have shown that it is likely that he did have some kind of relationship with a college-age au pair from whom, it is argued, he developed his taste for gold and jewels. She was beautiful, this woman, but she would not have sex with him, no matter how much jewelry he gave her. By the time he was sexually mature, she had left the family. This year of separation, known as the <u>Seminal Year</u>, is the time that Evans and Quiller cite as the year he developed <u>tripolarism</u>.[1] Always a fractious child, he now turned into a contrarian, self-centered adult who hated all women, and one might expect, both hated and wanted to suckle from his mother.

Juvenile Offender

God's first offense (breaking) occurred in -32, when he was 13. As a juvenile offender, he was given the lightest sentence — a month in a juvenile-offenders' house. His second offense, a more serious one (breaking and entering) occurred a week after release. He served another month in juvenile detention. A week after his release, he burned down his first townhouse and was sentenced to two years' imprisonment in a mixed adult/juvenile prison.[citation needed]

Skill-sets Develop

Although he worked in the license-plate stamping room as vocational training, this facility is where he is thought to have gained his skill in pyrotechnics, biological warfare, and geological catechlysmics.

Famous in the pen for having a leadership complex, he would take offense at all who didn't humor him, which included the guards, who had to be replaced often due to his habit of destroying them at a whim. This period of his life is when, according to Gulch, Trickett, and Gutapurna, God developed his lifelong habit of creating, setting, and scattering Indiscriminate Destruction Devices (plagues, earthquakes, and assorted Pain, Death, and Destruction).[2]

From Gang Leader to Institutional Director with a Global Reach

Known as <u>YHWH</u>, his slogan was from the beginning, "I am what I am." After a remarkably short time, his superb follow-through, never swinging an empty threat, gained him such a slavish following that his troops began to look upon him as "Father," the name he has risen with, and retained, even as his family has grown. Although his armies are uncountable, he has never maintained a personal guard, having demonstrated countless times that he enjoys taking care of himself. He has, it has been theorized, a secret source of power—something so central to his ability to punish and govern absolutely that if this substance were withdrawn, he could go into terminal arrest. (The substance is boiled <u>spinach</u>, an invention without rival in the days before <u>hormone enhancement</u>.) Shortly after his deportation to the planet in blue, after a particularly bad mood, he began to be referred to by those left alive as "the merciful," and he has been called that ever since as an additional assuaging title after he throws some disaster.

Globalization Brings Changes

Team members are being recruited now on all continents. [citation needed]

Other Health Problems

God was born with a film over his eyes, a condition known as Caulfield Syndrome. Although this cleared around age 14, his vision became more and more limited to a small field just in front of him, a dim one at that. This condition, known as _Tunnel vision (also known as "Kalnienk Vision"),_ still plagues him.

Nature or Nurture?

God is perhaps best known for his role in the evolution of the social sciences.

Although Mayhew concentrated on the London poor, who were frequently targets for God's crimes, neither Mayhew nor the great statesmen of his day paid any attention to this lone miscreant who remains as uncaught as Jack the Ripper. No one ever analyzed why they didn't include God in their attempts to guide society toward the social Good, though Patinka Mays Houghton postulated that since the great social reformers have always been the class with wealth, they don't want to waste their efforts on the unemployable, but they do need to reform the work force to their needs. [3]

Houghton, with his _Bow House, Work House_ sought to enter the debate. The book—a "revolutionary thoughtbuster," according to Alea Forceman, _New Statesman_—might have at least been reviewed in _New Scientist,_ if Yale Press had published it. Unfortunately, Little Red Press was only known in 1996 for publishing _The Secret Marxism of Bees_ and _Stories from My Vagina._

In 1945, B.F. Skinner (as lead scientist) was the first to draw the link between upbringing and behavior in the newsbreaking paper, "-45 to -40: The Formative Conditions that Made a Psycopath."[4] This study, citing years of animal testing, argued that the evidence was past hypothesis, that God's actions are the inevitable outcome of his neglected childhood (already proven by Freud to have damaged him from breast-feeding age, beyond any self-repair). Skinner died resenting the controversy this paper stirred up.[citation needed] He felt that his findings had been simplified and skewed, that he was summed up as a mere behaviorist, certain criminal elements taking the facts about God's incarceration and Skinner's conclusions to mean that criminal actions should not be punished, but positive incentives handed out instead.

In fact, the paper blamed much of God's personality problems upon his poor vision and stated that God does not just have tunnel vision, but can hardly see at all: thus the compulsion, during his mid-life crisis, to get an artificial light source to help him see for part of the time. That this light source would cause him pain is another breakthrough in realization that Skinner said he experienced as a gestalt (which led, according to Kcrzseiky, to Skinner's falling out with Sangstromm).[5] The paper further postulated that God suffers from photosensitivity, so that he can only tolerate so many lumens for a certain period of time without suffering halovision and the migraines that come soon after. Burr said in a BBC interview in 1978 that he is convinced that God's migraines have never been treated and that Burr's list of incidents caused by these migraines was cut from the paper without his permission, by Skinner, who blamed the JoB.[6]

Today, Skinner et al. are being undermined by advances in biotechnology. Many of the world's most prominently famous scientists are showing how we are "hardwired" and our future "programmed" by our genes.

Genealogy

God's grandfather on his father's side was a moderately successful traveling sustenance-salesman. God's father, an only child, was allergic to most sustenance, but liked the opportunities he had as a travelling salesman, so he sold something that didn't make him sneeze and that didn't weigh him down with product: encyclopaedia subscriptions. It is not known what their first and middle names were, but the family *God* is not one known on dwarf sub-planet 8943-P789 (which, linguistically, doesn't tolerate an unaccompanied *G*), though Kgod is common. One theory put forward in the *Pennington Journal of Incarcmigration* is that during processing upon arrival at the blue planet, prisoner number ? (the numbering system is unknown), Name: Kgod, ~#+* Joe Al, was entered in the Book, in the EZ to rite form: God. As the Book was lost in a fire shortly after God's arrival, not even his fingerprints survive.[7]

God's mother's maiden name was Jo-Beth @@@ (Appledaughter). Her family were fruit growers on both her father's and mother's side.[citation needed] God was the youngest child of countless siblings, his oldest sister As-Ura having the independent streak in the family. She left dwarf sub-planet 8943-P789 as soon as she could travel, a good illion and a half years before God was born. She traveled to the blue planet as an explorer, but when she arrived, put down roots, because what she saw was good. She seems to have had a very happy life here, dancing and singing and being quite a popular motivator. Back home, she had never been known for having their equivalent of a green thumb, but here on earth, she could just talk to a plant and it would spring forth, and she was positively dangerous to women who were tired of being fruitful, though she was great company, able to tell a joke and not laugh at her own punch line. However, within a year of God's arrival on the same planet as she'd lived on for so long, she was made the target of God's first great political purge. This was so successful that the only surviving relic we have of her habitation here is the first ironic word in earthly language: "insurance," meaning "promise to protect."

God: Tourist, Emigrant, Migrant?

At either the year 0 or 1, or thereabouts, God got the travel bug, according to his unauthorized biography *I Did It*.[8] Although there are no passports, manifests, or customs documents to prove any assertions, the <u>Earthipodean Society</u> was formed in 1912 to "spread the truth" about God having been judged an <u>Intransigent</u> and deported at age 45 to Earth, "for the term of his natural Life."[citation needed]

Whatever the reason he came, he has made Earth his home ever since, though he is such a recluse that *Time Magazine* put out an all-points bulletin on April 8, 1966, with their cover, "Is God Dead?" Although millions of people thought this was merely a late <u>April Fools' Day</u> joke, others realized that the influential journal was seriously asking people to search. These were the days before milk cartons performed that social service. The lack of a photo or even a police-artist's composite sketch has always made the search for the missing celebrity a difficult if not impossible mission, if finding him is the goal.

Bibliography

God is most famous for his "Ten Commandments," the document that forms the root of the word "tautology," and from which evolved the English higher-education word, "taught." Five of the ten demands are for unwavering and undivided respect, interrupting general life and other relationships.

Since that time many people claim to have been his ghost writer and others to have carried out their activities under his orders. [citation needed] But he has never written anything else that was such a blockbuster and that was purely his own invention, albeit dictated à la <u>Barbara Cartland</u>.

New Directions, Retraining

In January 2012 God was accepted as one of the new crop of students to be enrolled in <u>London University</u>'s first ever crime-writing MA.

Schedules of Enforcement

During the first year of God's incarceration in adult detention, he developed a personal code that he called his "Schedules of Enforcement." After attacking an officer or another inmate, he would explain that this attack was in accordance with his code and that any disruption to his enforcement of this code should only be so that his chosen lieutenants could act on his behalf. God had much trouble keeping order in the penal system of dwarf sub-planet 8943-P789, but has had no trouble on the planet in blue. It is the efficiency and willingness of his large force here that has given him the urge to become a bestselling author of what is hot: crime at the moment, although he considers himself primarily a poet.

Political Beliefs

As with many of the top conservatives since the 1980s, God has been very influenced by Friedrich Hayek, first being impressed by *The Abuse and Decline of Reason*, and then being absolutely blown away by *The Road to Serfdom*. God, however, finds the reasoning of most people influenced by Hayek to be fatally weakened by the human spirit. The logical conclusion of the need for less government because of its inherent faults is to do away with the root problem: human leaders, each seeking glory for self, funded with offerings from the people.

The Tea Party was formed by thinkers who understand half of the problem. The Wharton Tea Party site states: "God give us unalienable rights (His rights). God sets moral laws that govern 'we the people.' Governments exist to protect the rights God has given."[9]

God is happy, it is reported, that some of this common sense is finally getting around without his having to pound it into his followers' heads.[citation needed]

One institution that is helping to reform governance worldwide is The Ark-of-Salvation, which sells a book that he is said to have ghost-written.[citation needed]

"This book provides the antidote to the disease known as the 'New World Order.' The Bible says (Micah 4:1-5) that in the end, everyone will come to Jerusalem in the name of _his own god_. This provides the basis for an entirely different sort of 'new world order': one world under **God.**"[10]

God is pro-choice.[citation needed]

GF

The year numbering system used with <u>God Forevermore notation</u> was devised by God when he was still a juvenile. We know that because these notes scratched on the walls gave him an affection for this writing surface (instead of short-lived paper).[citation needed] No agreement has ever been reached as to the meaning of the system of GF, so no one has ever been able to date God's birth in relation to our system of time measurement. The only thing that's certain is that he was born on the 3rd of October, because he says so.[citation needed]

Notes/References

1   Kelvin Evans and Crody Quiller, _Orders and Disorder in the Pre-analytic World_, Vol. 3, Humanopsychtric Press, Edinburgh, 1999.

2   Sheldon H. Gulch, Manfred Trickett, and A.S. Gutapurna, "One Strike and You're Out: A Survey of Sentences Brought Down by an Advocatless High Court," _JIAJ_ (the _Journal of International Advocates for Jurisprudence_), (Oslo, 2007) vol. 54, pp. 10–32.

3   Patinka Mays Houghton, _Bow House, Work House: Why God Has Never Been Reformed_, Little Red Press, Oakland, CA, 1996.

4   B.F. Skinner, M. J. Oldevie, Wilbur W. Sangstromm, and Xavier Burr, "-45 to -40: The Formative Conditions that Made a Psycopath." _The Journal of Behaviour_, Issue 24, June 1963: 35–69.

5   Josef Kcrzseiky, *The Skinner Beneath*, Veracity Books, NY, 1977.

6   *Scandalous Behaviour*: *Real dramas in the lab*, an hour-long special report, 2 April 1978.

7   Ludmila Ogonsky, S.J. Chatterji, and Manuel Bourciez, "ID ~#+*; A Case of Autoformatting Abnormal Characters Highlights Our Need to Address Polycodal Personal Identity Reference," *The Pennington Journal of Incarcmigration* (Pennington Institute, Pennington, New York) Issue 1, Winter 2011: pp. 95–115.

8   J. Turber, *I Did It*, Houghton Miftin, Schenectady, NY, 1969.

9   http://www.whartonteaparty.us/Reports/Meeting%20Report%208-24-10.pdf.

10 http://www.ark-of-salvation.org/intro.php.

La Cucaracha Rules

Lucy Sussex

(!) This article has numerous issues, which attempts to rectify so far have been singularly if not spectacularly unsuccessful.

* It needs additional citations for verification

* It may contain original research

* May contain nuts (or not, depending upon your personal level of paranoia)

* All attempts to trace the author have failed

La Cucaracha Rules

The Moscow Rules is the term for rules of engagement supposedly developed during the Cold War by the Central Intelligence Agency, but certainly understood by covert agents on both sides. They are freely available in spy novels, or on the internet. Why and how the entry on them in Wikipedia was annotated by parties unknown we cannot say, but it was brought to our attention by the webmaster at ConspiracyTheory.com. Repeated attempts to delete the annotations led to continual reinstatements. As a result this new entry on Wikipedia was created. It has so far proved curiously unhackable.

List of Rules

• Assume nothing

That's a good one. Don't assume I'm just a hacker. Don't assume your head of government isn't a cockroach. We're all fellow travelers.

• Murphy is right

Yes, if anything can go wrong, it will. The last time was during the Cuban Missile Crisis. What a stuff-up! We had to cancel the victory celebrations.

- Never go against your gut; it is your operational antenna.

That's a fact. We knew it long before the scientific articles. When faced with information overload (i.e., everyday modern life) the human animal plumbs for unconscious decision-making. Which often can be dead right. How do you react when you see one of our unamalgamated selves? Do the dance, stomp, stomp, with your big feet, as if you know what we're up to. The only effective response is to mess with your antennas.

- Don't look back; you are never completely alone

Paranoia is an evolutionary survival trait: just because you're paranoid doesn't mean you're not prey. Stay alert, stay alive. One way we deal with it is to goad people into a state of mind where they're constantly paranoid. Thus they're inured, can't identify the real threat creeping up behind them. Grassy Knoll, giant alien lizards controlling the world, Protocols of Zion, you name it, we've created and road-tested it. Really messes with the antennas.

- Everyone is potentially under opposition control

See above.

- Go with the flow, blend in

I've been doing that as long as I remember. In the twentieth century alone I helped create mustard gas, messed with the stockmarket, was a particularly fervent Nazi, then an equally fervent Cold Warrior. I'm not telling you what I do now, but I very narrowly missed out on living in Abbotabad with Osama bin Laden. The poor sods who did get that gig complained that he snored, very loudly.

- Vary your pattern and stay within your cover

See above. Even if it is a burkha. But handy for those days when the amalgamation isn't at its best. Like bad hair days, only much much worse. From your point of view.

- Any operation can be aborted. If it feels wrong, it is wrong

Mid-'80s, we had a sick Soviet sub in the Atlantic, nuclear-powered, with a load of warheads pointing at the US eastern seaboard. Armageddon, go go go! At the last minute R&D produced a report that said nuclear wasn't the way. Too messy. Here's how to achieve optimum conditions for Apocalypse and all you have to do is wait. You'll see. The beauty was it required minimum effort, apart from a nudge here and there. I will admit we nudged Osama. And the Bush dynasty.

- Maintain a natural pace

That was what R&D said after '86. All the air travel, light bulbs, commuter cars, they add up over time. Before they know it, they'll have tipped over the critical point, no going back, heading for fossil-dom. But we seriously underestimated the pace of greed, which has got downright unnatural lately. So you noticed something was going on, after all? Which means we have more fun thinking up ways to make you trip over your feet.

- Lull them into a sense of complacency

Dead easy. What makes people complacent? Comfort food, and lots of it. Added bonus if it devastates the ecosystem and the human body. That's the Bread, and the Circuses are on the nearest screens: *Big Brother* and internet porn. Provide all in all answers, which just happen to be wrong. That's Religion™. If any sense starts being made, shout them down. Noise always wins. Look at Foxtel—but only with the sound turned down.

- Build in opportunity, but use it sparingly

Find those whose interests and yours just happen to coincide. Politicians are good, the ones who aren't amalgamations, of course. They've only got a few years of power, can't see beyond their feet. Or the next campaign fund check, never mind who it comes from. Before they know it, they've sold their souls to the corporations. Who are ours, all ours, body and soul. Why do you think they're so successful?

- Float like a butterfly, sting like a bee

Excuse me, that's speciesist. You don't have to choose the prettiest, or the ones whose values fit your preferred moral model: industry, productivity, capitalism writ small. For cryingoutloud, the bees haven't even evolved a hive mind! And they can't amalgamate, far less shapeshift. How about the ones who are good at hiding, running away, who watch and lurk from your kitchen shelving and under the floorboards? The ones who've got suspiciously very good lately at not getting squashed. And we haven't lost any legs either, despite what the song says.

- Don't harass the opposition

You harass us. We're just returning the compliment, but slowly and subtly. Viva la revolution!

- There is no limit to a human being's ability to rationalize the truth

Correction, irrationalize. You would think with all the fossil evidence, dinosaurs in the rocks, that science would be your god. Nope, there's a theme park in the US with a pair of Tyrannosaurs poking their heads out of <u>Noah's Ark</u>. Two by two? Two by down the big reptilian red lane, more like. Just because you're an idiot doesn't mean you can make Noah in your image. Here's another example: daffodils in fall. Cue chorus of hands-wringing and cries of "Oh, you can't mess with economic growth!" or "We can't lose money!" Always shuts down their brains.

- Technology will always let you down

That's the lesson you're learning, loser-species. And it's fatal.

- Pick the time and place for action

As I said before, inaction mostly, on our part.

- Keep your options open

Wonder why the NASA Mars probes have done so well? Well, just in case we over-egged the pudding, we've got a back-up plan. And no competition this time. <u>Curiosity </u>didn't kill us, nothing much does. Unlike you...

- Once is an accident. Twice is coincidence.
  Thrice is enemy action

Security breaches are rare. Once was in what would become the Czech republic, beginning of the last century. We still think must have seen something, but got it arse-backwards, anyway. That was Mr K's <u>Metamorphosis,</u> dismissible as fantasy. Twice was the time someone got drunk with an ex-CIA operative called <u>Alice Sheldon</u> in a seedy Washington bar. Talked too much, and got fictionalized as four crazy firemice from the planet Dirty. Speculating in NY real estate before the planet went anaerobic! Well, that last bit was right. Luckily it could be dismissed as <u>Science Fiction</u>. Three times is me, hacking into Wikipedia. Enemy action, you betcha, but against who? It might be the truth, the ultimate conspiracy theory. Or else just more pumping up the paranoia, the final messing with the human antennas.

Author Biographies

Alisa Alering was born and raised in the Appalachian mountains of Pennsylvania and now lives in the somewhat flatter environs of southern Indiana. She is a 2011 graduate of Clarion West and a 2012 winner of Writers of the Future. Her fiction is forthcoming from *Flash Fiction Online* and *Clockwork Phoenix IV*. She contributes the Writer's Room column to *Waylines* magazine. For more, visit http://alisaword.wordpress.com, or follow her on Twitter @ alering.

John J. Coyne is a writer and composer. He is a graduate of the 2011 Clarion West writers' workshop. He lives in New York City with his wife and daughter.

L. Timmel Duchamp is the author of the five-novel Marq'ssan Cycle and *Love's Body, Dancing in Time* and *Never at Home*, collections of short fiction, as well as the short novel *The Red Rose Rages (Bleeding)* and dozens of short stories that have been published in magazines and anthologies like *Asimov's SF* and the Full Spectrum and Leviathan series. Her fiction has been a finalist for the Nebula and Sturgeon Awards and short-listed numerous times for the James Tiptree Jr. Literary Award. Her essays and reviews have been published in numerous venues, including *The American Book Review, The New York Review of Science Fiction, Extrapolation, Foundation, Science Fiction Film and Television*, and *Strange Horizons*. She is also the founder and publisher of Aqueduct Press and the editor of *Narrative Power: Encounters, Celebrations, Struggles, Talking Back: Epistolary Fantasies*, and *The WisCon Chronicles, Vol. 1*, and co-editor, with Eileen Gunn, of *The WisCon Chronicles, Vol. 2*.

Kristin King is a writer, parent, and activist who lives in Seattle with her spouse and two children. Her work has appeared in *Strange*

Horizons, Calyx, The Pushcart Prize XXII (1998), and elsewhere. She has wanted to write a hyperlinked story ever since the 1970s, when she got to play text adventures on the mainframe at her dad's work. Somebody told her that if she finished the whole game she'd get to write part of the story, and so she spent a lot of time wandering through twisty mazes while drinking hot cocoa. Now she just writes the stories.

Catherine Krahe's fiction has appeared in *Realms of Fantasy, Futures from Nature, Ideomancer*, and *Daily Science Fiction*. She attended the 2011 Clarion West workshop and is staff for the Alpha Young Writer's workshop. Catherine lives in Iowa and plans to save the world by telling stories and planting trees.

Alex Dally MacFarlane lives in London, where she is pursuing a MA in Ancient History. When not researching ancient gender and narratives, she writes stories, found in *Clarkesworld Magazine, Strange Horizons, Beneath Ceaseless Skies, Shimmer* and the anthologies *The Mammoth Book of Steampunk* and *The Other Half of the Sky*. Poetry can be found in *Stone Telling, Goblin Fruit, The Moment of Change* and *Here, We Cross*. She is the editor of *Aliens: Recent Encounters*, out in June 2013 from Prime Books, and *The Mammoth Book of SF Stories by Women*, due out in late 2014.

Jenni Moody is a graduate of the 2011 Clarion West Writers Workshop and holds an MFA from the University of Alaska Fairbanks. Her stories are forthcoming or recently published in *Booth, Spring-Gun*, and *River Oak Review*. In 2013 she placed third in the Southern Writers Symposium Emerging Writers Contest. She's lived in a dry cabin in Alaska and a small town in Japan, and was once chased by a family of bears through the Yukon at midnight. She collects stamps (inked, not licked) and writes in the company of her two black cats in Huntsville, Alabama. She blogs regularly at jennimoody.com.

Mari Ness lives in central Florida, where she keeps a careful eye out for fairies, spirits and other local wildlife. Her fiction and poetry have appeared in such places as *Clarkesworld Magazine, Apex Magazine, Strange Horizons*, and *Daily Science Fiction*. You can find a longer length of her works at marikness.wordpress.com, or follow her on Twitter at mari_ness.

Mark Rich has written biography, literary criticism and cultural criticism. He used all three approaches in writing *C.M. Kornbluth*, his most recent book, and is employing at least two of them in his current, second book for McFarland & Co. The presses Small Beer, Wordcraft of Oregon, Fairwood, and RedJack have brought out collections of his fiction. He lives in the Coulee region of Wisconsin where he, life-partner Martha, and life-saver Scottie dog Sammy are auction-goers, junk collectors, and antique sellers. His many distractions of recent years have included a stint as winemaker at a regional winery.

Nisi Shawl's collection *Filter House* was one of two winners of the 2009 James Tiptree, Jr. Award. Her work has been published at *Strange Horizons*, in *Asimov's SF Magazine*, and in anthologies including *Dark Matter, The Moment of Change, Dark Faith 2*, and *The Other Half of the Sky*. Nisi was WisCon 35's Guest of Honor. She edited *The WisCon Chronicles 5: Writing and Racial Identity*, and *Bloodchildren: Stories by the Octavia E. Butler Scholars*. She co-edited *Strange Matings: Octavia E. Butler, Science Fiction, Feminism, and African American Voices* with Dr. Rebecca Holden. With classmate Cynthia Ward, Nisi co-authored *Writing the Other: A Practical Approach*. She is a cofounder of the Carl Brandon Society. She serves on the Board of Directors of the Clarion West Writers Workshop, from which she graduated in 1992. Her website is www.nisishawl.com. She likes to relax by pretending she lives in other people's houses.

Jeremy Sim was recently stuffed in a box and mailed to Germany, where he lives with his girlfriend Celine and their incredibly cute dog Rico. In 2011, he received the Octavia E. Butler Memorial Scholarship and attended Clarion West Writers Workshop. His short stories have appeared in places like *Waylines, Crossed Genres,* and *Flash Fiction Online.* When not writing, he spends his time playing video games, experimenting in the kitchen, and perfecting the thrilling technique of arriving at the platform just as the train pulls away. Visit his author website at www.jeremysim.com.

Lucy Sussex was born in New Zealand. She has edited four anthologies, including *She's Fantastical* (1995), shortlisted for the World Fantasy Award. Her award-winning fiction includes books for younger readers and the novel, *The Scarlet Rider* (1996, to be reprinted 2013). She has five short story collections, *My Lady Tongue, A Tour Guide in Utopia, Absolute Uncertainty, Matilda Told Such Dreadful Lies* (a best of), and *Thief of Lives.* Currently she reviews weekly for *The Age* and *Sydney Morning Herald.* Her latest project is *Victorian Blockbuster: Fergus Hume* and *The Mystery of a Hansom Cab* (forthcoming).

Anna Tambour is the originator of the forever vigilant ONUSPEDIA (motto: *An expert is someone who makes sure of the spelling.*) Tambour's latest novel is CRANDOLIN.

Anne Toole is a WGA-nominated writer for computer games, one-hour television, webseries, and short fiction. Her credits include the Streamy and IAWTV award-winning webseries *The Lizzie Bennet Diaries, Days of Our Lives, Stargate Worlds,* and the WGA-nominated dark fantasy game THE WITCHER. Due to her transmedia experience, Anne has spoken at the inaugural Nokia OpenLab 2008, GDC Europe, GDC Online, South by Southwest, the Login Game Conference, and Comic-con International. She also serves on the Los Angeles board of the International Games Developers Association (IGDA). Anne graduated from Harvard with an ever-so-useful degree in Archaeology, naturally. You can follow her on Twitter: @amely

Nick Tramdack was born in 1985. He attended the University of Chicago, where he wrote a BA thesis about Gothic novels. In 2011 he attended Clarion West, where he had the pleasure of meeting many other contributors to this anthology. His work has appeared in *Andromeda Spaceways Inflight Magazine, Shanghai Steam*, and *Three-Lobed Burning Eye*. He lives and works in Chicago and maintains an erratically updated blog at http://spectechnique.com. Among other projects he is currently developing a novel about gays, gods, and giant robots.

Big Mama Stories
Eleanor Arnason

Space is Just
a Starry Night
Tanith Lee

Squaring the Circle
Gheorghe Săsărman

Strange Matings
edited by
Rebecca J. Holden
& Nisi Shawl

The WisCon Chronicles, Vol 7
Shattering Ableist Narratives
edited by JoSelle Vanderhoof

Feminist Voices:
The Best of Femspec
edited by Batya Weinbaum